(Original Title: Tink in a Tangle)

Too Much Trouble

by DOROTHY HAAS

Pictures by MARGOT APPLE

Cover by RICHARD WILLIAMS

SCHOLASTIC INC.
New York Toronto London Auckland Sydney

For Helen and June
and Treasured Memories

Reading level is determined by the Spache Readability Formula. 2.2 signifies high second grade level.

ISBN 0-590-41117-9

Text copyright © 1984 by Dorothy F. Haas.
Illustrations copyright © 1984 by Margot Apple.
All rights reserved. This edition published by Scholastic Inc.,
730 Broadway, New York, NY 10003,
by arrangement with Albert Whitman & Company,
publishers of the book under the title TINK IN A TANGLE.
LUCKY STAR is a trademark of Scholastic Inc.

12 11 10 9 8 7 6 5 4 3 2 1   6 7 8 9/8 0 1/9

Contents

1
Daughter of the Harvest Moon

Tink pressed her nose against the window at the Fountain of Beauty. She cupped her hands around her eyes so she could see better.

Inside, pink net curtains hung at the windows. A sparkly glass lamp hung from a gold chain above a white fountain. Water bubbled from it, sparkling, never stopping. The beauty shop was a very glamorous place.

And Tink's mother was a very glamorous lady. Tink could see her inside the shop combing out a woman's hair.

Tink pushed open the door. Cool air washed around her. It felt fresh after the outdoor heat, and she shivered happily. The Fountain of Beauty had to be cool because air from the hair dryers was hot.

She went to her mother and leaned against a

shelf, looking at herself in the mirror. Red hair! Ick!

"Mom," she asked, "will you color my hair?"

Her mother didn't look up. She kept on combing the lady's hair. But she laughed. "No, I will not color your hair. You're too young."

In the mirror, Tink watched her mother work. Comb-comb-comb. Pat-pat-pat. It looked easy, the way her mother did it. The lady's streaked hair was beginning to be very glamorous.

"Well..." Tink opened one of the fancy bottles on the shelf and sniffed. Yummy! "How old do I have to be before I can color my hair?"

"Sixty," said her mother. "You'll have to say, 'Mom, now can I color my hair?' I'll check out your wrinkles. And then maybe I'll decide you're old enough and maybe I'll say yes."

The lady in the chair laughed loudly.

"Aw, Mom," said Tink. Her mother definitely was not taking this problem seriously. "Red hair's terrible. It always gets me in trouble."

"Don't 'Aw, Mom' me," said her mother. "Run over to the shampoo bowl and ask Miss Winnie to wash your hair so I can cut it."

Tink liked Miss Winnie. Miss Winnie talked to her as though she was grown-up.

While she soaped Tink's hair, Miss Winnie talked about her grandson. "He's got his letter for basketball," she said. She went on telling about him while she rinsed Tink's hair and rubbed it dry. "He's smart as can be. Why, he likes things like geometry. He'll get a basketball scholarship to college and get himself a good education. He'll *be* somebody someday."

Tink was certain of that. Geometry sounded hard. Anybody who liked it was sure to be famous.

Miss Winnie ran a comb through Tink's wet hair and dropped a pink towel around her neck. "Scoot, now. You're all set for your cut."

"Thanks, Miss Winnie," said Tink.

Her mother was still busy with the woman in her chair. Tink stopped at the low table in front of the dryers. She always liked to look at the magazines. They were very glamorous. The beautiful women in them wore furs and jewels and gorgeous dresses.

Today there was something different on the table, an old-looking book with swirly gold letters on the cover. The words were hard to read, but at last Tink figured them out: *Mrs. Ione Tuttleby's Hints for Happiness, or, How to Dip into the Sugarbowl of Life.*

She flipped through the book. There was only one picture, at the beginning. It was a drawing of a lady with piles of wavy, curly hair around her face. It was a very old-fashioned picture.

The first part of the book had lots of long pages filled with printing. Tink always looked for the talking parts in books. Nobody was talking to anybody in this one. The rest of the book looked sort of like a dictionary. All the *A* things were first. Then came the *B* things, and so on. Acorn. . . dentist. . .guitar. . .music. . .nuts. . .

Her eyes fell on the word *coins*. She read:

> To see someone counting out coins means
> you will one day be rich.

Neat! She knew where she could see someone counting coins. All she had to do was go to the check-out counter at Columbo's Supermarket.

Under *bird* it said:

> To see a bird with beautiful feathers means
> you will wear beautiful clothes.

Why, she only had to go over to Lincoln Park Zoo to see birds with beautiful feathers! Did that mean she might get some gorgeous new clothes? What a great old book!

"Tink," called her mother. "I'm ready for you."

Dragging her feet, looking at the book, she went to her mother's chair. The lady with the streaked hair was gone. Her mother was shaking out the pink sheet that had covered her.

"Mom, look at this funny old book," said Tink.

Her mother glanced at it. "Oh, that old thing. Someone left it here months ago. It's nutty nonsense."

"If it's been around here a long time, maybe nobody wants it," said Tink. "Can I have it?"

"Ask Miss Lorna," said her mother. "She's the boss. Now put it down and climb up here."

Tink put the book on the shelf. She settled herself in the chair with a bounce. Her mother pinned the pink sheet around her, put the top of her hair in a clip, and began cutting the sides.

Tink stared at herself in the mirror. She was all covered in pink. "You always say pink is death on redheads. I don't think I look so awful. I love pink."

9

"Mm-mmmm." Her mother was only half listening. "I like you in cool colors—green like your eyes, or blue. Someday you'll be pretty in gray. Now stop wiggling or I'll nip your ear."

Tink did her best to sit still. "I just don't see why I have to have red hair," she groaned. "Poppy's hair is brown. Lisa's is the color of sand."

"And your father's hair is red," said her mother. "Do you suppose that has something to do with it?" She slipped her fingers through Tink's hair and held it out beside her ears. "I think I'll cut it a little shorter this time." She started cutting again.

"I wonder what that book says about red hair," said Tink. "Red hair is a terrible problem. When you've got it, trouble follows you like. . . like ants going after sugar."

Her mother laughed. "Your hair is not a jinx," she said.

"What's a jinx?" asked Tink.

"Something that causes bad things to happen," said her mother. "Your hair is pretty. It makes you different from other people."

"I'll say it does," said Tink. "It makes more trouble for me." She thought of what had happened

10

yesterday when she was playing with her best friend, Poppy.

"Do you know how Mrs. Flower is always trying to get the twins to stop sucking their thumbs? Well, I got this really great idea. I told Chryssie and Daisy there was a tooth troll under the front porch and if they didn't stop sucking their thumbs—"

"A what?" asked her mother.

"Tooth troll," said Tink. "I made it up. I told them he's the bad cousin of the Tooth Fairy and if they didn't stop sucking their thumbs he would come in the night and take away their teeth and not leave them any dimes."

"You...are...a...stitch!" said her mother.

"Well," said Tink, "today Mrs. Flower said the twins had bad dreams last night, so I had to tell them it was all make-believe. And it was such a good story—such a good spooky. I know if I didn't have red hair, I wouldn't have got in trouble with Mrs. Flower."

Her mother put her hands on Tink's shoulders and looked at her in the mirror. "Just how do you figure all that ties in with red hair?"

"Because I get these great ideas, and they always turn into such—such *trouble*," said Tink. "It happens when you've got red hair."

"What I think," said her mother, "is—you do things without thinking. Then you don't want to be responsible for what you've done. When you were little you blamed things on that invisible friend you had. 'Freddie made me do it,' you'd say. Two years ago, you thought all your troubles happened because your father didn't live with us anymore. Now it's red hair."

Tink groaned. Nobody—not one single person—understood about red hair.

Her mother went on. "Your hair is pretty."

"Isn't," said Tink.

"*Is,*" said her mother. "It's the color of a new penny. Remember what old Mrs. Wing Yee calls you? Daughter of the Harvest Moon." Snip-snip-snip. She cut some more. Snip.

The name did sound pretty, even though Tink didn't know what the words meant. She said them aloud. "Daughter of the Harvest Moon.

"What's a harvest moon?" she asked.

"The moon when it's golden orange in the fall," said her mother. "That's when farmers pick their corn and pumpkins."

"Oh." Tink thought of something else. "Can we stop at the House of Wing and get a carry-out dinner?"

Her mother fluffed Tink's hair. Then, watching what she was doing in the mirror, she blew the hair dry. It all looked super easy.

"There," said her mother. "That's better. You were beginning to look like a shaggy mutt. Now you're set for school. It'll be starting soon."

She shook out the pink sheet. "Okay, let's have chicken chow mein. We haven't had it for a long time. Anyway, I think we've only got a jar of pickles at home in the fridge."

"I want an egg roll," said Tink, climbing down from the chair. "Can we get fortune cookies, too?"

"Mmm-mmm," said her mother, tidying up. "I'll be ready in a minute."

Tink picked up *Mrs. Ione Tuttleby's Hints for Happiness* and went looking for Miss Lorna. Surely Miss Lorna wouldn't want an old book like this in her glamorous beauty shop.

2
Tink's Great Idea

Summer was coming to an end. Tink and Poppy had done every single thing there was to do.

They were at Tink's house. The TV was turned on to a game show, but they weren't watching.

Tink's legs were over the arm of her chair. Her cat Willy was on the floor beside her, playing with a ball. A bell inside the ball tinkled every time he batted it. Tink dropped her hand and smoothed Willy's silky fur. Willy batted the ball and darted out from under her hand.

Tink yawned and stretched and smoothed back her hair. It felt nice when it was just cut—light and airy. And then she got an idea.

She looked across the room at Poppy. "I know what let's do!"

Poppy looked up from the orange beads she was stringing into a necklace. "What?"

Tink bounced to her feet. This was the absolute best idea she had ever had. "Let's have a beauty shop! You can be Miss Poppy. You'll wash everyone's hair, and I'll put rollers in it or blow it dry. I'll be Miss Tink."

Poppy dropped the orange beads into her denim craft bag. A beauty shop? "Zowie," she said. "I never heard of anything so much fun!"

Tink led the way into her mother's bedroom. "Our customers can sit here at my mom's dressing table and look into the mirror while I make them glamorous."

The glass top of the dressing table was covered with fancy bottles and jars. The mirror above the table was framed in gold. The bench in front of it was covered with puffy gray velvet.

"It's gorgeous," sighed Poppy. "Someday I'm going to have a dressing table just like this."

Tink got out a comb and a brush. She found some rollers for setting hair and put them on a chair next to the bench. "There," she said. "I can pick them up just the way my mom does."

In the bathroom, she set a bottle of shampoo on the sink. "You can wash people's hair here," she

16

said. "We've got gallons of this. My mom gets it free at the shop.

"Now," she went on, "after you wash a customer's hair, you put a towel over her shoulders and you comb out the tangles. Then you say, 'You're ready for Miss Tink,' and you send her to me."

Poppy was looking around the bathroom. "Everything about your house matches." She sighed. "Your towels don't even have any mends. This is a very glamorous bathroom. Our house isn't one bit glamorous."

Tink did think the bathroom was pretty. The walls were papered gray and gold, and her mother had painted the outside of the old tub pale gray with a border of gold leaves. There was a jar of little red rosebud soaps and a big jug of bubble bath. The towels were bright red. And it was true—not one of them was mended. Lots of things at Poppy's house were mended.

Tink thought of something nice to say. "But your house is cozy. If it's snowing and your mother's baking cookies, your house is the best place in the whole world. I like your cozy house."

"I like your glamorous house," said Poppy.

They went back to planning the beauty shop.

"What'll we call it?" asked Poppy.

Tink frowned, thinking hard. A beauty shop had to have a beautiful name. "There's the Ginger Jar on Broadway. A lady named Ginger owns it."

"And there's the Pink Ribbon on Clark Street," said Poppy. "That's a pretty name."

Tink bit her lip. She thought of the shops around the Fountain of Beauty. Mr. Wing Yee called his restaurant the House of Wing. Her face lit up. "We could call it the House of Tink! No—that sounds funny."

"How about Tink's House of. . .of Hair?" asked Poppy.

"House of Gorgeousness," said Tink. "Tink's House of Gorgeousness!" Tink's House of Gorgeousness sounded just right. It sounded glamorous.

Tink remembered other things they would need. "When people call for appointments, you write their names down. I'll get a notebook."

"I'll make some ads," said Poppy. "We can take them around to everyone."

18

While Poppy drew the ads, Tink gathered up magazines and stacked them on the coffee table. "Here's where people will wait," she said.

"Mm-mm-mm," said Poppy. She sat at the dining-room table, frowning as she drew.

Tink got towels out of the bathroom closet. She got a mug from the kitchen so Poppy could use it to rinse the customers' hair. She set it by the bath-room sink. There. The bathroom looked just right.

She found her mother's blow dryer in a drawer in the dressing table. There was another dryer in the closet. It had a cap to cover rollers while warm air blew them dry. She put the dryers on the chair next to the dressing table.

What else did she need? She thought of the things her mother used at the Fountain of Beauty. A sheet. She would put it around the customers' shoulders while she worked.

She found a sheet that had red flowers on it. There!

Poppy came to the bedroom door. She held up the ad. It was printed in red Magic Marker. "I'm going to outline the red with purple," she said. "Won't that be glamorous?"

Tink read the ad.

BE GLAMORUS
VISIT
TINK'S HOUSE
of
GOR-JUS-NESS
Hair Washed   Hair Fixed
CALL NOW FOR AN UP-POINTMENT

"Wow!" said Tink. "That's just great! I'll help make some more just like it, and then we can take them around."

They made six ads and a sign that said "Open" for the door. Then they ran downstairs and outside. They left one in Maria's mailbox, another in Sue's, another in Lisa's, and one more in Erin's. There were two left.

"What'll we do with them?" asked Poppy.

"Let's tape them to the lampposts in front of Mr. Frickensmith's store," said Tink. "That'll take care of anyone we missed."

"What if a grown-up lady sees the ad and comes?" asked Poppy. She looked a little scared.

Tink giggled. "Wouldn't that be a stitch?"

3
Jane Ellen

Tink and Poppy went back to Tink's house. While they were eating chocolate-chip cookies and drinking orange pop, the telephone rang.

"A customer!" Tink set down her glass.

"Who's going to answer?" Poppy swallowed her last bite.

"You are! You are!" Tink was excited. Imagine! A real customer.

"What'll I say?" wailed Poppy. "This is your house. You're supposed to answer the phone."

The telephone kept on ringing.

"But you're supposed to make the appointments," said Tink.

"I write 'em down," said Poppy. "But that doesn't mean I have to answer the phone."

They darted to the living room. Tink picked up the telephone. "Tink's House of Gorgeousness," she said, trying to sound grown-up.

A giggle came over the line.

"I know you," Tink said. "That's you, Lisa Owens. And you're not supposed to laugh."

"I would"—Lisa swallowed a giggle—"would like to make an appoint"—another giggle—"appointment for me. And one for Sue, too. And we want to come right away. Our hair's a terrible mess."

"One . . . moment . . . please." Tink had heard Miss Lorna say that once. She turned to Poppy. "Lisa and Sue want to come now," she whispered. "Can you fit them in?"

"Well, of course," said Poppy. "Nobody else has called yet."

Tink spoke to Lisa. "You may have our first appointment," she said. "But you'd better hurry because we are going to be very busy today."

Lisa giggled again and hung up.

"And that's all there is to it," Tink said. "See? It's easy."

Poppy wrote the girls' names in her book.

"Lisa gets the first appointment," said Tink. "That's because she called for both of them."

The telephone rang again.

Poppy grinned at Tink and picked it up. "Tink's House of Ab-so-lute Gorgeousness." She listened for a minute. "One...moment...puh-lease," she said. "It's Maria," she whispered to Tink. "She wants to know if we do fingernails."

Tink spun on her toes. Her idea was turning out better than she had ever thought it would. "Do we do nails? Tell her we do fingernails and toenails, too."

Poppy gave the message to Maria and wrote her name in the book.

"My mom's got all this gorgeous nail polish," said Tink. "Red Ginger and Dragon Plum. She's even got gold."

The next caller was Erin. "Can you give me curls?" she asked Tink. "I don't even have to bring Dawn with me," she added. "My mom's taking her to the doctor for a shot."

Dawn was Erin's little sister. Their mother thought sisters should do things together. Dawn followed Erin everywhere.

Tink was thinking. Erin's black hair was straight as wet noodles. "Golly," she said, "I don't know about curls. But I'll sure try."

That made four appointments. Everyone who had gotten an ad had called up the House of Gorgeousness.

When the telephone jangled again, they both stared at it.

"The ads on the lampposts!" said Poppy. "I'll bet some lady saw one. What'll we say? You answer."

Wondering, Tink picked up the phone. "Tink's House of—"

A sob came over the line.

Tink held her hand over the receiver. "Oh, no. We forgot Jane Ellen!"

"It was mean-mean-mean of you to leave me out!" said a teary voice. "I saw you put ads in everybody's mailbox—"

"And she's crying," whispered Tink.

"She told me she always gets what she wants by crying," Poppy whispered back.

"—so I went outside and looked at the ad in Sue's mailbox. And—" Jane Ellen's voice droned on.

"We really don't want to hurt her feelings," whispered Poppy.

"Besides, if we don't let her come, she'll do something really awful to us," whispered Tink. "Like the time she put ants in our lemonade." She put the phone back to her ear.

"You're horrible not to invite me. So there." The words ended in a wail.

"Hey, Jane Ellen," said Tink, "I guess we sort of overlooked you. You can make an appointment if you want to."

Jane Ellen's voice changed instantly. "I can?"

"Sure," said Tink. "Come at three o'clock. What do you want done?"

"Just make me gorgeous," said Jane Ellen. Now she sounded blissfully happy. "I'll start out right away so I won't be late."

Tink hung up the phone. "She's leaving now"—her voice started to shake—"so she won't"—she fell over on the sofa, laughing—"be late!" The last word ended in a shriek.

Poppy doubled over, laughing. "But, but—she only lives across the street!"

4

Tink's House of Gorgeousness

The customers didn't come for their appointments one at a time. They came all at once. The buzzer sounded, and when Tink pushed the downstairs door release there was the sound of running feet on the stairs.

The feet stopped on the landing outside Tink's door. Poppy and Tink could hear a lot of whispering and giggling.

Sue's voice came through the door, reading the sign: "Tink's House of Gorgeousness. Open."

"Does that mean they are open?" asked Erin. "Or does it mean we're supposed to open the door?"

"Open!" Lisa commanded, giggling. The door burst open and the girls tumbled into the room, laughing.

"Me first!" shouted Maria.

"You said I could have your first appointment," said Lisa.

"But I beat you up the stairs. I got here first," said Maria. She held out her hands. "My nails are almost long. I haven't bitten them for two weeks. They'll be gorgeous with polish on them."

"I want to look gorgeous," said Sue. "But remember that my baseball cap has to fit on me whatever you do."

Erin lifted her long, straight hair away from her face. "Will it take a long time to give me curls? I'd better be first."

Jane Ellen's hair was an unruly mop. "I want long, puffy, wavy hair," she said dreamily, "like a country-western singer."

"Wait. Wait. WAIT!" Tink yelled above all the talking.

Everyone quieted down.

"Now, you must call me Miss Tink," said Tink. She turned to Poppy. "And this is Miss Poppy. You must call her that."

"Why?" Erin looked puzzled.

"Erin, don't always ask why-why-why," said Tink. "That's just the way it is. Everyone in a beauty shop is Miss Somebody.

"And there's something else," she went on.

27

"You've got to sit around reading those magazines until your appointments."

"Can't we watch you?" asked Erin.

"No," said Tink.

"Then can we watch TV?" asked Jane Ellen.

"That's okay," said Tink. "Or you can talk to each other about your glamorous lives."

"Come on, Lees," said Poppy. "Your name is first in my book."

Lisa followed Poppy to the bathroom. Tink scooped up Willy and went after them.

Lisa knelt on a stool in front of the sink. Poppy wet her hair, poured shampoo on it, and rubbed it into a pile of bubbles.

Tink sat on the edge of the tub, smoothing the little cat's soft fur, watching them. "You're too quiet, Lees," she said. "You're supposed to talk to Miss Poppy."

"Okay," said Lisa. "Miss Poppy, stop getting soap in my eyes."

"Not like that!" said Tink. "You're supposed to talk about what you're wearing to a party tonight. Or, ask Miss Poppy about her new bracelet."

Lisa giggled. "Tonight I'm going to McDonald's

28

with Timmy O'Brien and I want to look gorgeous. . .oooh, you're getting soap in my eyes. Miss Poppy, I really like your bracelet. Is it antique plastic? Hey, the water's too hot. . .oooh," she yelped, "now it's freezing."

Poppy rubbed Lisa's wet head with a red towel. "Okay. Now you can sit down and I'll comb it."

Lisa sat on the stool. "I did a lot of talking, but you're not saying anything. Isn't she supposed to talk, too?" she asked Tink.

"You should hear the stuff people talk about at the Fountain of Beauty," said Tink. "Sometimes they stop talking when I come near."

So Poppy talked as she combed out Lisa's tangles. "This bracelet used to be my mom's, so it's really old—it's an antique." She tugged, and Lisa screwed up her face. "It's real, genuine plastic—"

"Ouch!" shrieked Lisa. "You're hurting my head."

"I'm nearly done," Poppy said soothingly. "There."

"Now you come with me," said Tink.

Poppy went to get her next customer, and Lisa followed Tink into her mother's bedroom.

Tink put Willy down and pinned the flowered sheet around Lisa's shoulders. Then she combed Lisa's hair, looking at her in the mirror the way her mother looked at customers. "Mmmm," she said, "I think..." She pulled Lisa's hair into two ponytails, one above each ear. "I know what I'll do. I'll blow it dry. Then I'll put in two clips and make each end into a curl."

"Ponytails?" asked Lisa. "But ponytails are for little kids."

"Not with scarves," said Tink. "And perfume." She had just thought of the perfume.

"Perfume?" asked Lisa. "What's that got to do with it?"

"We always add perfume," said Tink, "to make you feel special. Timmy O'Brien will like it."

"Timmy O'Brien," Lisa said sadly. "Don't I wish! I mean, he doesn't even *not* like me. He doesn't know I'm alive."

Tink found it hard to hold the hair blower and comb out Lisa's hair. Funny! It looked so easy when her mother did it. But at last she had the hair nearly dry.

She parted it in the middle and fastened the two

bunches with rubber bands high above Lisa's ears. Some of the hair got tangled in the rubber bands.

Lisa moaned softly. "It sure hurts to be gorgeous."

Tink brushed the ends into two curls, looking at Lisa in the mirror.

Lisa looked disappointed. "I don't feel gorgeous," she said.

"Wait," said Tink. She went through the drawers of the dressing table. Colored scarves spilled onto the floor. At last she held up two pale blue pieces of nylon. "These will be just right. But you'll have to give 'em back when you go home."

She tied them in place, and suddenly Lisa did look prettier.

Tink handed her a mirror, saying, "Very sweet," the way she had heard Miss Winnie say it.

She picked up one of the bottles on the dressing table. "Mmm," she said, "here's my favorite. It's French and I can't say the name." She dabbed some of the perfume behind Lisa's ears. "There."

Lisa turned her head this way and that, smiling at herself in the mirror.

"Next," called Tink.

She needn't have called, for Sue was standing beside her, waiting to take Lisa's place on the gray velvet bench. Tink glowed. A beauty shop was the best idea! She had never had so much fun!

"Remember about my baseball cap when you fix my hairs," Sue said seriously.

"Your *hairs?*" asked Tink. "Sue, nobody says *hairs!* It's *hair.*"

Sue shook her head. "I read in a book that I've got a hundred thousand hairs on my head. Everyone has. So please fix my hairs."

Tink looked at her, puzzled. She knew Sue was wrong, but she couldn't explain why. Oh, well. . . .

Sue's short hair lay on her head like a shiny brown cap. There wasn't much Tink could do with it except blow it dry—and Sue looked exactly the way she always did. Tink tried to make up for that by putting some blusher on Sue's cheeks.

Sue wrinkled her nose. Then she tried on her baseball cap. "Hey! All right!" she said.

But Tink still wasn't satisfied. She looked through her mother's makeup. "Eye shadow—you need some of this," she said, adding purple powder to Sue's eyelids.

Sue was looking more glamorous by the minute.

Tink's eyes roamed over a row of lipsticks at the back of the dressing table. "How about some of this?" she asked. She held out Party Pink.

But Sue liked TNT Red. She put it on herself.

Tink finished by dabbing perfume behind Sue's ears.

"Put some on my nose," said Sue.

"You don't put perfume on your nose," said Tink.

"I do," said Sue. "How else will I smell it?"

Erin was waiting to be next. She nudged Sue aside and plopped down on the velvet bench. "Curls," she said.

It was very hard to make Erin's long hair stay on the rollers, but at last Tink got all the rollers wound. She put the cap of the old dryer around Erin's head and showed her how to turn it on. "You'll have to sit and read magazines while you dry," she said.

"I can hardly wait," said Erin. "Curls—real curls!" She trailed into the living room, the cord of the dryer dragging after her.

Then while Poppy put polish on Maria's fingernails—Maria chose Dragon Plum—Tink pinned the flowered sheet around Jane Ellen's shoulders.

She combed through Jane Ellen's mop of wet hair. "You know, Jane Ellen," she said thoughtfully, "You might look nice with bangs."

"Really?" said Jane Ellen. "I've never had bangs."

"I think bangs would be very interesting," said Tink. "Shall I give you bangs?"

"Well," said Jane Ellen, "if you think so."

"I think so," said Tink. She found her mother's scissors. She remembered how easily her mother cut her hair. *Snip, comb, snip, comb.* There was nothing to it.

She combed Jane Ellen's hair down over her eyes. Then she snipped it straight above Jane Ellen's eyebrows. Easy!

She stepped back and looked. One side seemed shorter than the other.

She combed a little more hair down over Jane Ellen's eyes. This time she tried to make all of the bangs match the short part.

"My bangs look crooked," said Jane Ellen.

"They just need a little even-ing up," said Tink.

34

She spoke in her most sure-of-herself voice. But a funny feeling was starting somewhere in her middle.

She evened Jane Ellen's bangs, and she evened them some more. Then she stepped back and looked at them again. Some of Jane Ellen's hair stuck out straight, high above her eyebrows. And there was a kind of upside-down V above her nose.

"I look funny!" Jane Ellen's voice came out in a squeak.

Tink reached out her comb. "I'll just—"

"You won't 'just' anything!" Jane Ellen jumped up. Hair flew off the flowered sheet. "You're making me look terrible. You're not making me gorgeous at all and I want to go home."

"Let me cut a little on the side," said Tink. How could she let Jane Ellen leave the House of Gorgeousness looking as though she had been caught in a street sweeper? "Maybe a little on the—"

Jane Ellen was tugging at the sheet. "Don't you touch me again with your old scissors, *Miss* Tink." Tears spilled down her cheeks.

Tink unpinned the sheet.

"You didn't want me to come." Jane Ellen hiccupped. "You're mean, mean, mean."

The girls gathered around her.

"Oh, Jane Ellen," said Poppy. "Tink didn't cut your hair wrong on purpose."

"Yes, she did," sobbed Jane Ellen. "She's got ugly hair and she wants me to be ugly, too."

Tink felt as though a black cloud had settled around her. Everything was all wrong. She had not meant to make Jane Ellen look horrible. She reached for the perfume bottle. "Let me put some perfume behind your ears."

Jane Ellen knocked the bottle out of her hands. It fell to the floor. A dark stain showed on the carpet. A smoky sweetness filled the air.

"My mother says you're a redheaded troublemaker," yelled Jane Ellen. "An ugly redheaded troublemaker!"

She ran from the room. The front door slammed. The girls heard her running down the stairs.

"Wow," said Lisa softly.

"Her bangs did look kind of strange," said Sue.

"I cut my hair once, when I was a little kid,"

said Erin. "My mom spanked me."

"What'll your mother say about the perfume?" Maria asked Tink. Holding her fingers stiffly, she picked up the perfume bottle.

Poppy tried to make Tink feel better. "Her hair will grow out. Hair always does. That's the nicest thing about it. And see how gorgeous everyone else looks?"

Tink looked around. Lisa, with her ponytails and scarves, did look pretty. All that eye shadow made Sue's eyes look mysterious. Maria was the only kid on Greenbrier Street with Dragon Plum fingernails. And soon—Tink was hopeful—Erin was going to have curls.

But—what would her mother say?

5
"Melissa Catherine..."

It didn't take Tink long to find out.

She and Poppy were alone, and Tink was still scrubbing at the stains on the carpet with a wet towel when the bedroom telephone rang. She sat back on her heels. She didn't want to answer that telephone!

Poppy came to the door carrying an armful of soggy towels. "Maybe you better not answer. It might be Jane Ellen's mother."

Tink groaned. "That would be *luck*. I think it's *my* mother."

Poppy handed the ringing phone to Tink.

"Hello?"

"Melissa Catherine Becker, what in the name of common sense have you been doing there?"

Tink shut her eyes. Melissa Catherine—that meant bad trouble. "Nothing much," she said. "Just having fun."

"Fun!" Her mother's voice rose. "Fun?" Tink held the phone away from her ear. "Clare Moore just called and said you'd hacked off her beautiful child's hair."

"I didn't hack it." Tink was hurt. "I was really careful, only she wouldn't let me finish. And I didn't cut it all off. I was just giving her bangs. She might look better with bangs."

"Melissa"—a long sigh came over the line—"whatever you did, Clare is furious. She's bringing Jane Ellen in after my last appointment this afternoon so I can fix the damage."

There was a pause. "Who...else's...hair... did...you...cut?"

"Nobody's," said Tink. She was thankful about that.

"Melissa"—her mother still sounded mad—"I have a feeling you didn't stop with just Jane Ellen. You get carried away. What else have you been do- ing there today?"

Tink told her about the House of Gorgeous- ness—all except the perfume. When her mother found out how good the house smelled, maybe she wouldn't be too mad about the spilled perfume.

"Everyone except Poppy went home a while ago," Tink said. "They really did look gorgeous."

Someone spoke to her mother in the background and Tink heard her say, "I'll be right there." Her voice came over the phone again. "I'll find out the rest when I get home. Now you clean up any mess you've made. Take the towels to the laundromat. Then Poppy is to go home and you are to stay inside till I get there."

"Okay, Mom," mumbled Tink.

She hung up. She knew more scolding was to come. "Why do I get such good-terrible ideas?" she moaned. "I mean, why do my good ideas get me into such terrible trouble? Oh, if only I didn't have this awful, horrible red hair. Only people with red hair have so much trouble!"

"The House of Gorgeousness was fun while it lasted," said Poppy. "Everybody had a good time, except Jane Ellen."

"If only she'd let me cut a little bit more," said Tink. "Maybe I could have fixed things."

Poppy used the vacuum cleaner to get Jane Ellen's hair off the carpet.

Tink put away all the beauty shop stuff. She got

the detergent out of the back hall closet. Then she climbed onto a chair to get laundry change out of the cupboard.

She stood on the chair, counting quarters and dimes. Should she take enough to buy ice-cream cones? An ice-cream cone would be very comforting.

Then she thought of what her mother would say when she discovered extra money missing from the laundry mug. She climbed down from the cupboard and got green Popsicles out of the freezer. Green Popsicles were almost as comforting as ice cream, and they were free if you got them from home.

Tink and Poppy headed down Greenbrier Street, licking the Popsicles, carrying the soggy towels.

"Ick," said Poppy. "My T-shirt's getting all wet. Why did we use so many towels, anyway?"

"Don't know," said Tink. "They just do, in beauty shops. Every time they do something to your hair—zap, there's another towel around your neck."

Suddenly Poppy stopped. She stared at Tink.

"We forgot about us! You didn't do my hair. I didn't wash yours."

They giggled, leaning against a lamppost.

"Tomorrow," said Tink. "Come over tomorrow and I'll do your hair. That is, if I'm not grounded and can have company."

They walked on. "You know, " said Poppy, "I'd really like to have nice, floppy straight hair."

Tink studied Poppy's headful of dark curls. A wicked gleam came into her eyes. "Why don't I cut a little bit around—"

"Ha!" said Poppy, laughing. "Ha!"

Later, upstairs all by herself, Tink put away the stack of red towels and the flowered sheet. She turned on the radio in the kitchen and got another green Popsicle. Then she turned on the TV in the living room to make things cheerful.

Willy frolicked around her feet. Tink picked him up and cuddled him against her cheek. Willy reached up his pink tongue and licked the Popsicle.

"Hi Willy," said Tink. "Nice old cat. Doesn't it smell good in here? I hope Mom thinks so."

The telephone rang. It was her mother again.

"You didn't call me at four o'clock. Remember the rules? You check in at twelve and four, no matter where you are."

"But I was at the laundromat," explained Tink. "And anyway, you've already scolded me this afternoon."

"No excuses," said her mother. "Now you stay inside until I get home."

"Okay, Mom."

Tink hung up, feeling terrible again. She looked at the empty Popsicle stick. And there weren't even any more green Popsicles in the freezer to comfort her.

6
Best Friends?

"Mom, you can't mean that!"

"You can just bet I do," said Tink's mother. She had started talking as she came in the door. She dropped into the big red chair in the living room. "Call Jane Ellen tonight and offer to take her to McDonald's for a hamburger tomorrow."

"But what if she wants a Big Mac? And fries? And a shake, too?" wailed Tink. "It'll take all my savings."

"You weren't thinking when you cut the poor kid's hair," said her mother. "This will help you to remember to think ahead."

Tink curled up in a corner of the red sofa. "It looked so easy when you cut my hair," she moaned. "And I wasn't going to cut much — just some bangs."

"It looked easy," said her mother, "because I went to beauty school and learned how to do it."

"We were all having so much fun," sighed Tink, "until Jane Ellen got mad. She said I've got ugly hair and I wanted to make her ugly, too."

"Your hair is not ugly," said her mother.

"Is," said Tink.

"Isn't," said her mother. "You look just like your dad. He's not ugly, is he?"

"He's handsome," said Tink. "Did he always get into trouble? Is his red hair a jinx? Is that why you're not married anymore?"

Her mother shook her head. "I've told you—we were too young to get married. Much too young. And no, he didn't always get into trouble. And he has good ideas, too—like going to Alaska to work in the oil fields. Someday he'll be rich. Then he'll do nice things for you."

"I wish he was here now," said Tink, "and he was rich, and I was rich, and I didn't have to use up my savings on Jane Ellen." She made a face. "She said her mom says I'm an ugly redheaded troublemaker."

"Sounds to me like Jane Ellen made that up,"

said Tink's mother. "I really don't think Clare would say such a thing."

"Jane Ellen makes up lots of stuff," said Tink, "and it's always mean. She told Poppy that Mrs. DeLuca, our craft teacher, said she put icky colors on things. Poppy felt bad. So I asked Mrs. DeLuca if she really said that, and she didn't."

"Did Poppy make something nicer than Jane Ellen?"

"Yes," said Tink. "Poppy's dish was prettier."

"Jane Ellen was jealous," said her mother. "Well, anyway, don't be mean back to her." She sniffed. "Ugh. The house simply reeks of perfume."

"But it's a good reek," Tink said hopefully.

"That perfume was my favorite." Her mother looked sad. "Something tells me I'm never going to want to smell it again."

Tink's mother went off to try to clean the perfume out of the carpet and Tink rolled over onto her stomach and reached for the telephone.

Jane Ellen answered on the first ring. She sounded bouncy, not the least bit like someone whose life has been ruined.

"You mean just you and me?" she squealed

when Tink invited her to McDonald's. "And Poppy won't be coming, either?"

"Just you and me, Jane Ellen." Tink closed her eyes. It was going to be awful. "Just you and me," she said gloomily. "I'll meet you on your steps at noon."

She hung up, feeling terrible. She had to buy a hamburger for someone who said she had ugly hair. And her very best friend wasn't even going to be there to make things better. Poppy never had money for things like hamburgers. She always had to eat at home.

Tink wandered into her bedroom and threw herself down on the fuzzy white rug next to her bed.

She thought about good ideas that turned into tangles of trouble.

About making Jane Ellen look ugly.

About being an ugly redheaded troublemaker.

About not being able to wear pink because her mother said it was death on redheads.

She pulled a loose thread on the dust ruffle on her bed, thinking. Darn. . . old. . . red. . . hair. . . .

Suddenly her eyes fell on the corner of a book

almost hidden by the dust ruffle. A red book with gold letters on the cover. She pulled out *Mrs. Ione Tuttleby's Hints for Happiness*. She could use some happiness! She propped her head on her hand and dipped into the Sugarbowl of Life.

> More is known than wise men have written. People of the past had sayings of deepest meaning. To wish upon the first star of evening meant the happy outcome of that wish. To accidentally let a fork fall meant a friend would come to call. And, of course, everyone knew that daisies don't lie.

Mrs. Tuttleby didn't say what that meant. Maybe everyone knew about daisies. He loves me . . . he loves me not. . . .

The print was small and hard to read. Tink moved ahead a few pages.

> The point, my dears, is to look for the happy signals in life. Seek out those things which hold promise of happiness for yourselves.

"Hey, neat," thought Tink. She turned the pages to the dictionary part of the book, to *R*. Was there anything about red hair?

Mrs. Tuttleby had lots to say about redbirds

and red foxes and red ribbons. But there wasn't a single word about red hair.

"I knew it," thought Tink. "Red hair's not one of the good things in the sugarbowl of life. I've been telling Mom that practically since I was born."

What about *hair*, then. Did Mrs. Tuttleby say anything about just plain hair? Tink turned to the *H*s.

Aha! there was something about hair.

> To see a woman with golden hair is to know
> that a great surprise awaits you just around
> the corner.

Lisa's hair was blonde. Was that the same as golden? Hey! She had just seen Lisa. Did that mean there was going to be a surprise, maybe?

> To see someone with long, curling locks
> means happiness in love.

Maria's big sister was going to be married soon. Tink wondered if she had seen someone with long, curling hair.

Tink read on. The book was fun. It would be neat to look for things that would bring happiness. It would be fun to dip into the sugarbowl of life.

When her mother left for work the next morning, she warned Tink, "Be nice to Jane Ellen. You've got your watch? Don't forget to call me at twelve and four no matter where you are. Ugh! I can't stand the perfume smell," she said on her way out the door. "I'll have to pick up a rent-a-cleaner this afternoon."

Tink promised. Her nose wrinkled. There really was too much perfume in the house. Even her cereal, Count Chocula, tasted like perfume.

The bell rang soon after her mother left. Tink leaned out her bedroom window to see who it was.

Sue had her bat and ball. "We're getting up a game," she called. "Want to play?"

"You bet," called Tink. She slammed the window and ran downstairs.

Poppy and Lisa and Maria and Erin were there. But not Jane Ellen.

"You never know whether she's going to be nice or mean," said Sue.

"Sometimes lately she acts like she's thinking of being nice," said Maria. "The other day at craft class she didn't push ahead of anyone."

"Do you think maybe she's going to change?" asked Erin.

"If she does," said Poppy, "I hope it's soon."

"Let's get going," said Sue, "before she sees us."

"Maybe there'll be some boys at the park," said Lisa. "Maybe they'll want to play."

The boys had their own game. But Sue found some more girls, and they played ball all morning.

Tink was up at bat twelve times, and she didn't strike out once. It was Sue who saved the game, though. She hit a home run with the bases loaded. They won—twenty seven to twenty three—just before it was time for Tink to run home and call her mother.

Poppy ran beside her.

"I wish you could come with me to McDonald's," said Tink. "It's going to be terrible, just me and Jane Ellen."

"I can't," said Poppy. "My mom says we can't spend our money that way. But, hey—maybe this'll be a day when Jane Ellen's trying to be nice."

"Hope so," said Tink as they got to her house. "I sure hope so."

Tink checked in with her mother. She washed her face and hands and the elbow that was dirty. She put on her third best pair of jeans and her striped T-shirt and went to meet Jane Ellen.

Jane Ellen came running downstairs, her face lit up with smiles.

Tink stared. Gone was Jane Ellen's mop of wild hair. Soft curls framed her face. Curls at the sides. Curls around her ears. Wispy curls on her forehead.

Jane Ellen whirled in front of Tink. "Your mom made me look really nice. She said my hair just needed to be cut right."

"Wow, Jane Ellen," said Tink. "You look gorgeous." And she meant it. She really did.

The badness was gone from Jane Ellen's face. Her mouth turned up instead of down at the corners.

"I'm sorry I said you have ugly hair," said Jane Ellen. "Your hair really isn't ugly at all."

Jane Ellen was apologizing! Jane Ellen never apologized. Maybe she really was changing, as Maria had said. Tink gulped. "That's okay, Jane Ellen."

She chattered all the way to McDonald's. "I've always wanted to be friends with you, Tink. But you were best friends with Poppy."

Tink didn't know what to say. Was she best friends with Jane Ellen now, just because they were going to McDonald's together? She talked about something else. "School starts next week. I wonder who our teacher will be?"

"I've got a new dress for school," said Jane Ellen, "and new shoes, and new notebooks. Next week I'm going to get new felt-tip pens, and—"

"I guess everyone will have new stuff," said Tink. Jane Ellen bragged a lot about the new things she got. Jane Ellen couldn't stop being Jane Ellen all at once!

At McDonald's Jane Ellen only wanted a plain hamburger, not a Big Mac. And she ordered a Coke instead of a shake. Her lunch was cheaper than Tink had expected. She began to feel better.

Jane Ellen bit into her hamburger. She looked seriously at Tink. She swallowed and said, "You're really nice to buy me a hamburger, Tink. And I want to say thank you for cutting my hair, too."

Tink's mouth opened. Then she remembered she had food in it. She finished swallowing. "You do?" She couldn't believe what Jane Ellen had just said.

"Yes," said Jane Ellen. "Because if you hadn't made a mess of my hair—"

Tink sighed. That again.

"—if you hadn't cut it wrong, my mother never would have taken me to your mother, and your mother would never have cut my hair like this, and I would never have felt so *gorgeous!*"

She squealed the last word.

Three boys at the next table rolled their eyes. They got up and left.

"Did...you...see...those...boys?" whispered Jane Ellen. "They were looking at me. I think they like me!"

New hair-do—same old Jane Ellen.

Jane Ellen did look surprisingly cute. And she was, almost, nicer. But—did Tink want her for a best friend? No! Never!

7
Double Trouble

Tink didn't have to spend the next week—the very last week before school began—worrying about having Jane Ellen for a best friend. Jane Ellen went to Wisconsin to visit her grandma and grandpa. And Tink did her best to stay out of trouble.

One afternoon, Sue's mother took everyone to see the Cubs play ball. It was Helmet Day and they all got free batters' helmets.

Sue put hers on saying, "I'm going to wear it every day, even when I'm not playing ball."

Another day Poppy's mother was extra busy and Poppy had to look after the twins. Tink was helping her.

"We're supposed to keep them out of the sun," said Poppy.

Tink fanned herself. "I'm melting, it's so hot. Why don't we turn on the hose and let them play in the water?"

The twins heard. They took their thumbs out of their mouths, looking very interested.

"What a good idea!" said Poppy. "But we'll have to watch them."

The hose lay in the front yard like a long, green snake. Poppy turned on the water and fixed the nozzle so it made a light shower. She held the hose, and the twins hopped around, screeching.

"Let me hold it," Chryssie begged after a while.

"No, me, me," said Daisy.

Tink and Poppy looked at each other.

"Oh, why don't you let them hold it," said Tink. "They can't get any wetter than they already are."

Poppy gave the hose to Chryssie. "Remember, now. Take turns."

The little girls sprayed each other. Their squeals were loud enough for a whole nursery school.

Poppy coaxed her cat Nilly out from under the front porch. Nilly had scooted there when the water came on. "Come, Nilly," Poppy said soothingly.

Tink was reading Mrs. Tuttleby's book. "Listen to this, Popp," she said. "'Twins are a sign of double good fortune. To see identical twins means—'"

An ear-splitting shriek came from the sidewalk.

Tink and Poppy looked up.

Chryssie was spraying Daisy. Or maybe it was Daisy who was spraying Chryssie. Whichever twin it was, she was also spraying a very dressed-up woman walking along the sidewalk.

Tink grabbed the hose and turned it off.

"I'm so sorry," gasped Poppy.

"Humph," said the woman. She marched through the gate, up onto the porch, and rang the doorbell. Water dripped from her hair. It dripped from her dress in a wet ring around her feet.

Mrs. Flower came to the door. "Oh, my dear!" she exclaimed. "Let me get you a towel. Let me put your dress into the dryer."

"Those children," snapped the woman. "The little ones can hardly be blamed. But the big girls should have known better." She glared at Tink and Poppy.

Mrs. Flower looked past the woman, to Poppy. "Take the twins to the backyard to play. And watch them this time," she warned.

Tink and Poppy each took a twin by the hand and went around the side of the house. As they went, they heard Mrs. Flower say, "Do come in.

You can blow-dry your hair. And you can wear one of my shifts while your dress is drying. Would you like some iced tea?"

Tink and Poppy sat on the edge of the sandbox. It was very boring watching the twins pour sand from one pail into another. But Tink and Poppy didn't take their eyes off the little girls.

"Mrs. Tuttleby says twins are a sign of double good fortune," said Tink.

"Ha!" said Poppy. "They are a sign of double trouble."

"Mrs. Tuttleby says to see identical twins means two good things are going to happen to you."

Daisy threw sand at Chryssie. Chryssie threw sand back.

"Hey!" said Poppy. "Stop that. Leave the sand in the sandbox."

"Why don't you ride your Big Wheels?" suggested Tink.

The twins ran for their tricycles.

"Gonna race," said Chryssie.

"I'm gonna win," said Daisy.

"Stay beside the house where I can see you," Poppy called after them.

"Those Big Wheels make so much noise we'll sure know where they are," said Tink.

Nilly ran to get out of the twins' way. Poppy picked him up.

"Listen to what else Mrs. Tuttleby says about twins," said Tink. "'To see twins dressed alike in their old age is a sign that you will have a long life.'

"And here's another. 'To see brown-eyed twins means you will pass whatever test lies in your future.' Wow! Chryssie and Daisy have the brownest eyes I've ever seen."

"School starts next week," said Poppy. "I'll look at the twins every morning before I go to school."

The twins! Where were they?

There was no more noise from the Big Wheels. The twins were nowhere in sight.

Tink dropped Mrs. Tuttleby's book and followed Poppy. They ran.

Around the side of the house.

No twins.

Down the front walk.

No twins.

Onto Greenbrier Street. And there were the Big

Wheels standing on the sidewalk in front of the Whalens' house.

The little girls came skipping out of the Whalens' yard. Daisy was holding a golden flower as big as her head. "Look what we found," she chirped. "We're taking it to Mama."

"Oh, no," wailed Poppy. "You stole a flower."

"Didn't steal it," said Chryssie. "Picked it."

"Come with me," said Poppy. "You're going to have to apologize to Mr. Whalen."

She marched them to the Whalens' front door and rang the bell.

"When Mr. Whalen opens the door you say, 'We're sorry we picked your flower.' Say it for me. Say it now."

Chryssie and Daisy looked at each other.

"But we're not sorry," said Chryssie. "It's a pretty flower."

"It's for Mama," said Daisy.

The door opened. Mr. Whalen filled up the doorway. He looked down at them through the screen.

"My little sisters want to say something," said Poppy. She sounded scared.

Tink stood close to her. It was the best you could do, stand close when your friend was in trouble.

"Yes?" said Mr. Whalen. Then he saw the flower. His face got very red. "My prize dahlia," he said in a low whisper.

Poppy poked Chryssie. "What do you say?"

"We're sorry we picked this pretty flower," said Chryssie. She didn't look one bit sorry.

"We picked the flower for our mama," said Daisy. "But if you like it, we'll give it to you." She smiled sweetly and offered it to him.

Mr. Whalen closed his eyes as though he was praying. Then he looked down at his prize flower. "Thank you for telling me," he said. His voice sounded choked. "You may keep the flower for your mama."

He stepped back and closed the door firmly.

Daisy smiled brightly up at Poppy. "See? He didn't care."

Chryssie looked equally pleased. "He said we could keep it."

"We've got to tell Mom," said Poppy. She looked very unhappy.

Tink and Poppy each took the hand of a twin. With their free hands they pulled the rattling Big Wheels. They marched into the yard and back to the kitchen door. But they didn't go in.

The wet woman was now a dry woman. She was also a smiling woman. She was just standing up from the table. "Such wonderful gingerbread," she was saying. "Could you part with the recipe?"

Mrs. Flower moved with the woman toward the dining room. "That's a family recipe, handed down from mother to daughter. But I do have a delicious recipe for orange nut bread that nobody else has. Perhaps you'd like that."

The two women disappeared, talking.

Poppy opened the door. "Inside," she hissed to the twins.

"What's your mom going to say?" whispered Tink. She nearly tripped over Nilly as he followed them inside.

The front door closed. After a while Mrs. Flower came back into the kitchen. She was carrying Poppy's baby brother, Little Woody. She stopped, her eyes on the flower in Daisy's hand.

"This is pretty, just like you, Mama," said Daisy.

"It's a flower just for you," said Chryssie. "We picked it," she said proudly.

Mrs. Flower sank into a chair. She put her cheek against Little Woody's head. "Indeed, it is a flower," she said. "It's Mr. Whalen's prize dahlia."

She looked sternly at Poppy. "How did this happen?"

Poppy explained, as best she could. She told about ringing Mr. Whalen's doorbell.

"And he said we could keep it," said Chryssie.

"He said we could give it to you," said Daisy.

"Thank you very much," said Mrs. Flower. "But you may not take things that do not belong to you."

"Didn't take it," said Chryssie. "Picked it."

"Picking and taking mean the same thing when a flower is in someone else's yard." Mrs. Flower sounded very patient. "We'll talk about it later." She looked up at Poppy. "Get them out of those sandy clothes and pop them into the bathtub. And then you can watch them in your room, please, for the rest of the afternoon."

Tink sniffed the gingerbread. She was drowning in the nose-tickling smell of gingerbread. Her mouth was watering for gingerbread.

Mrs. Flower looked at the pan on the stove. Two squares were gone. "Well, there goes our dessert," she said. "I'll take it next door to Mr. Whalen, along with the lemon sauce."

"No dessert for dinner?" asked Poppy.

"Applesauce," said her mother.

Tink sighed. She felt sorry for Poppy, for all the Flowers, for herself. Nobody was going to get any of that yummy gingerbread today.

She scooped up Nilly and followed Poppy toward the stairs. And she couldn't help thinking.

The twins got into an awful lot of trouble without any help from anybody. But today she had helped them.

Playing with the hose was a really good idea. But then it had turned into trouble.

Riding the Big Wheels should have been okay. But that had turned into trouble, too—trouble not only for the twins, but for Mr. Whalen and for all of the Flowers. Nobody was going to have gingerbread for dessert.

"It's this terrible red hair," she thought. "It *is* a jinx. It causes bad things to happen. Not just to me, either. To everybody near me. It's catching!"

8
Surprise

Everybody came back from vacation. On the first full day of school, Sue and Lisa and Maria and Erin met Tink and Poppy in front of Poppy's house to walk to Chester P. Armbruster together.

Jane Ellen came running to walk with them. "There's a town near my grandpa's," she panted, "with all these great little stores. There's a sweet shoppe—that means a candy store. And I bought something for everyone."

She held out a wrinkled white bag. "It's maple sugar candy," she said. "They make it from the sap of trees."

Jane Ellen really was trying to be nice.

The girls all crowded around her and reached into the bag for the tan, leaf-shaped candy.

"Yummy!"

"It melts in your mouth."

"If you took a bite of a maple tree, would it be sweet?" Erin wondered aloud.

"Go ask a woodpecker," said Poppy. She giggled, but everyone else groaned.

Jane Ellen broke in. "I bought something special just for Tink and me."

"Oh, no," thought Tink, "what's Jane Ellen going to do to me now!"

Jane Ellen held up a round, gray thing. "It looks like a rock," she said. "The kind with pretty colors that you don't see till someone cuts it in half. Only"—she sounded important—"this is candy. See what happens when you lick just one side?"

She pulled half of a "rock" from her pocket. The flat, licked side had wavy circles of red, purple, pink, white, and blue.

"Ooooooo," said everyone.

Jane Ellen handed the unlicked rock to Tink. "This is just for you," she said.

Tink wanted to shrink. She wanted to become the amazing, shrinking girl and just disappear. But she remembered to be polite. "Thank you, Jane Ellen," she said stiffly. "It'll be a lot of fun to lick this."

She put the candy rock into her pocket, and they went on to school.

Jane Ellen walked beside Tink and Poppy for a while. Then she ran on ahead to show the others her new gym shoes.

Tink whispered to Poppy, "I think I'm going to just die! I don't want Jane Ellen to bring me special presents. I don't want this old rock, no matter how pretty it is. And I don't want Jane Ellen for my best friend."

"My mom tells me kids outgrow things. Maybe Jane Ellen will outgrow wanting you for a best friend."

"But *we* won't outgrow each other," said Tink. Suddenly she thought of something. "Hey! We'll take turns licking the rock." She began to feel better about the candy rock in her pocket.

"But not in front of Jane Ellen," whispered Poppy.

Nobody played much in the school yard. Everyone looked sort of shiny in brand-new school clothes. The kids crowded around the door, and when the bell rang they pushed inside, talking and calling to each other.

The very first person Tink saw was the custodian, Mr. Swenson, looking as grumpy as ever. He stood at the top of the stairs, leaning on his broom.

"He needs some good fortune, I think," Tink whispered to Poppy. "I should lend him Mrs. Tuttleby's book."

The old school smelled fresh and new, like floor wax and paint and varnish and pine-tree soap. Mr. Swenson might be grumpy, but he took very good care of Armbruster. He called it "my" school.

Tink felt funny, walking past her old room and not going in. She stopped and peeked inside. A new teacher was writing her name on the chalkboard.

"The kids all look so little," Tink said.

Poppy thought so, too. "Do you suppose we ever looked that babyish?"

Tink shook her head. "Not us," she said. "Not you and me."

Their room was down the hall, on the other side.

Mrs. Kincaid, their teacher, stood behind the desk. "Be seated, everyone," she called. "Anywhere will do. I'll assign seats in a little while."

Mrs. Kincaid was new at Armbruster. Tink had seen her when they registered for school. That day she had worn a red blouse. Today she had on red earrings, and there was a red handkerchief in her pocket.

"I wonder if she'll be nice," whispered Tink.

Mrs. Kincaid clapped her hands. "All right, everybody. Settle down. You there, next to the door. What did you say your name was? Timmy? Please close the door, Timmy."

On Mrs. Kincaid's desk were stacks of new books, waiting to be given to everyone. The chalk in the chalk trays was all long and new. There were new posters on the bulletin board.

Tink wondered what hard things they would be learning this year. And she wondered how far her seat would be from Poppy's.

As things turned out, Tink was in the second seat at the front. Poppy was in the same row, but at the back, and that was terrible. Jane Ellen was two rows away from Tink, in the middle of the room. That was good!

The first weeks of school passed. Jane Ellen stood in line next to Tink whenever she could, and showed her pictures in her reader, and talked to her a lot. Poppy was always there to make her feel better, though. And Jane Ellen didn't bring Tink any more presents.

There were hard new things to learn. But Mrs. Kincaid made them interesting. Everyone had to make up a game that used math problems. "You'll have until Christmas to finish your games," she said. "You can give them away for holiday presents."

TJ fell out of his seat laughing.

"I won't give you my game for Christmas," Tink promised Poppy. "I hope Jane Ellen doesn't give me hers!"

One evening, at home, Tink's mother kept looking at the clock.

"Are you going out?" Tink asked suspiciously. "You didn't tell me you were going out tonight." Tink hated being home alone at night. Even though the Cremers were at home on the floor below, she hated it. Even though the Petersons were always at home in the first floor apartment, she hated it.

"Yes," said her mother. "But there's no reason to fuss, because—"

"Who's fussing?" yelled Tink.

"—because we're going out together."

Tink blinked. She forgot about being upset. "We are?"

"Uh-huh."

"Where?" asked Tink.

"It's a surprise."

"When?" asked Tink.

"Now," said her mother. "Put a sweater on under your jacket. The nights are getting cool."

Tink ran for a sweater. When she came back, her mother was already wearing her own jacket. Tink ran downstairs and had to wait for her mother at the front door.

"No need to hurry," said her mother. "We've got plenty of time."

"Time for what?" asked Tink as they went outside.

Her mother grinned. "Not telling," she said. "Surprise."

Tink walked backward, looking up at her mother. "Is the surprise as big as my fist?"

"Bigger," said her mother.

"Lots?"

"Lots."

"As big as a house?" asked Tink.

"Oh, it depends on how you look at it," said her mother, laughing.

"Give me a hint," begged Tink.

"You've heard all you're going to hear from me," said her mother.

"You always do this to me," said Tink.

"Do what?" asked her mother.

"Take me places and don't tell me where we're going," said Tink.

"Oh, come on now," said her mother. "Aren't surprises fun?"

Tink was dying of curiosity. But she had to agree. "Yeah, fun."

She loved being out at night. The air was cool and damp on her face. The streetlights made shadows under the trees, and Greenbrier Street seemed mysterious.

Broadway at night was very different from Broadway during the day. The streetlights pushed away the darkness, making the street greenish bright. The stores all had lit-up signs in the windows. Only the windows of Chester P. Armbruster were black and dark.

Tink and her mother didn't stop in any of the stores. When they got to Thirty-One Flavors, Tink thought the surprise might be an ice-cream cone. But they went right on past. And anyway, an ice-cream cone was not as big as a house.

They turned onto Belmont Avenue and walked past apartment buildings. At Sheridan Road they waited for the lights to change to green.

Tink bounced up and down in suspense.

They crossed two more streets, waiting for the lights each time, and at last they came to the harbor. Only a metal link fence separated the sidewalk from the water. Her mother leaned her arms on the fence.

The harbor was filled with sailboats. Even in the darkness Tink could see the sails wrapped neatly around the tall masts.

Tink stuck the toes of her shoes into the links of the fence and raised herself up. She put her arms on the top of the fence, next to her mother's. "Is this the surprise?" she asked.

"No," said her mother. "You won't have to wait long, though."

Behind them, cars swished past on the Outer Drive. Horns sounded. Tires screeched. In front of them, the masts of the sailboats rocked gently. Below their feet, water slapped at the stones under the sidewalk.

"I like the wet smell of the water," said Tink.

"So do I," said her mother.

Tink looked past the sailboats, beyond the harbor, out to the darkness of the lake. "Something's way out there," she said, pointing. "I can see a light. Is it a ship?"

Her mother stared out into the darkness. "I can see it, too."

People walked past in back of them on the sidewalk. People in the boats called to each other. Tink watched and listened and waited.

"Hey, that's funny," she said after a while. "The ship out there is getting brighter. It almost looks like it's on fire. Is it coming to shore?"

Her mother didn't say anything.

Tink squinted at the light. Something about it was different. It grew bigger, more orange. It seemed to be curved. "That sure is a funny ship," she said.

"Don't you know what it is?" asked her mother. "It's not a ship."

"It isn't?"

"It's the moon," said her mother.

Tink looked at the moon rising out of the dark lake. It was reddish orange. Slowly it became more round. Its light made a glowing orange path on the water.

"It's a harvest moon," said her mother. "Since you're a daughter of the harvest moon, you ought to know what one looks like."

They stayed at the fence, watching, as the moon rose into the sky. It hung there, a glowing orange ball.

"It sure is beautiful," whispered Tink.

Her mother smiled.

"I sure like surprises," said Tink.

9
Slumber Party

It was Erin's birthday. Everyone was invited to her slumber party—even Jane Ellen, because Erin's mother said it would be hurtful not to invite her. And everyone had to think of a good game to play. "So we won't get bored," said Erin.

Tink and Poppy went to Erin's house together. They carried their sleeping bags and Erin's birthday presents.

"I hope we'll dance," said Tink. "I love to dance."

"What's your game?" asked Poppy.

Tink grinned. "You'll see," she said. "I really worked hard on it." And she had, too. She had even practiced, to make it come out right.

Erin buzzed open the downstairs door as soon as Tink rang the bell. She was standing in the doorway of her apartment when Tink and Poppy ran up the stairs. She was already in her pajamas—new red-and-white striped ones.

"Hi-eee!" she shrieked. Then she looked shy when Tink and Poppy gave her their birthday presents.

"What do you say, dear?" asked her mother.

Erin asked a question. "Can I open them now?"

"Now, do you think that's what I meant?" asked her mother.

"Uh—thank you very much for these nice presents," said Erin. She just stood there, holding them.

"Don't you think it might be fun to open them when everyone gets here?" asked her mother. "Why don't I take them for now?"

Erin looked relieved. She led the way to the living room.

Erin's little sister, Dawn, was smoothing out her sleeping bag right in front of the TV. She had on blue pajamas. On the back were the words *Kiss Me—I'm Cute*.

"Mom," wailed Erin, "nobody will be able to see TV with Dawn in front of it."

"Dawny," said Mrs. Lawson, "don't you think it would be nicer next to the bookshelves?"

"No," said Dawn.

"Nobody should be right in front of the TV," said Mrs. Lawson. She picked up the sleeping bag and put it in front of the bookshelves.

Dawn's lower lip stuck out.

The doorbell rang.

"Somebody else's here," squealed Erin. She ran to the hall. Dawn scampered after her.

Tink dropped her sleeping bag in front of the sofa. This was a fine spot, just fine. She reached into her sleeping bag and took out her little hand-held tape recorder. Quickly she slid it under the sofa. She grinned, thinking about her game.

"What did you put under there?" whispered Poppy.

"It's part of my game," whispered Tink. "I guess it's okay for you to know—I thought of the best spooky to tell. Only I made it really fancy. Wait'll you hear!"

Poppy unrolled her sleeping bag next to Tink's. She pulled out her nightgown. It was pink flannel with pink braid ties at the neck and wrists. "Let's get undressed right away," she said.

Tink looked longingly at the nightgown. "Your mom makes you the most ab-so-lutely great

80

clothes." She sighed. "I wish I didn't have red hair and I wish I *did* have pink clothes."

"My mom bought a million yards of this pink stuff at a sale," said Poppy. "I've got a nightie. She made the twins p.j.'s. I'm going to have a shirt. My grandma's getting a nightie. Pretty soon we'll all hate pink."

Tink held up her own pajamas. They were made of a pale green shiny material.

Poppy's eyes opened wide. "Are those real, genuine nylon?"

"Yup," said Tink. Just the way Poppy said that made her feel a little happier about her un-pink pajamas.

The rest of the girls tumbled into the room.

"Zowie," gasped Sue. "You look slithery, Tink."

"You've got lace!" Maria said wistfully. "You look glamorous. Look at mine. Just look!"

She held up a pair of blue pajamas. They had feet in them—and a fluffy bunny tail on the back.

"And this," she added. She held up a matching blue cap. It buttoned under her chin and had droopy rabbit ears. "My mother won't let me grow up," she groaned.

Everyone giggled. But they felt sorry for Maria, too.

They all unrolled their sleeping bags — then rolled them up again because there wasn't any room left on the floor.

"We wouldn't be able to dance with them out," said Tink.

"Or do gymnastics," said Poppy.

"Or play our games," said Jane Ellen.

"Look. Here comes the food," whispered Erin.

Mrs. Lawson set down several big bowls of popcorn. She kept going out and coming back with more food. Chocolate chip cookies. Potato chips. Tortilla chips. A bowl of olives.

"I love olives," said Erin. "Yummy."

Last of all Mrs. Lawson brought in a tray filled with all kinds of pop.

"Wait till you see my birthday cake," said Erin. "That won't come until later."

They munched and sipped and tried everything. Then they played the games.

"We'll do each game for ten minutes," said Erin.

But the first game only took a minute.

Lisa held up an egg. "We need tablespoons for this," she said.

Erin ran to get them.

"We've got to hold the spoons in our mouths and pass this egg from one person to the next. You've got to be careful. If you drop it—yuck!"

The egg didn't even get from Maria to Sue.

Everyone screamed when it fell. But the egg didn't splatter. It bounced.

"Rats," said Lisa. "I wanted the game to go on longer."

"You said it would break," said Jane Ellen. She sounded disappointed.

"That was to scare you," said Lisa. "My mom made me hard-boil it."

Sue's game was balloon bounce. Using their heads or elbows or knees, they had to keep a balloon in the air. Everyone bounced the balloon upward, like a volley ball.

"Keep it up. Up—up—up!" yelled Sue. She sounded just like Miss Whipple, their gym teacher.

The balloon didn't stay up. It landed in a lamp on top of the TV set and popped.

Poppy's game was the most fun. They all tied

balloons to their shoes. Then they jumped around, trying to stamp on each other's balloons and to save their own.

The room was filled with stamping and banging and popping. The game took a long time. At the end, Tink was the only one left with a balloon.

Maria's game was telling jokes and riddles. Only the trouble was, the girls all knew the same ones. That game ended in a hurry.

Jane Ellen's game was bubble blowing. She had brought bubble gum for everyone. They chewed and chomped and blew to see who could make the biggest bubble.

Jane Ellen won. Jane Ellen could make bigger bubbles than anybody. They all knew that when they started. But Jane Ellen didn't know that her bubble would burst all over her face.

"Jane Ellen, you won. Only you sort of lost, too," said Sue. "I mean, how are you going to get all that gum off your face?"

"Ick," said Jane Ellen, trying to pick a gooey string of gum out of her hair. "I guess it'll have to wear off."

She looked unhappy.

"Tink, what's your game?" Lisa asked. "Is it—a spooky?" She looked hopeful. "I love your spooky stories."

Tink had been waiting for this. She plopped down on the floor, her back against the sofa. "For my game, we have to turn off the lights."

"It *is* a spooky!" Lisa shivered happily.

"I don't like lights out," said Dawn.

"Baby," said Erin. She got olives from the bowl. The olives had holes in them and she stuck one on each finger. "So I can find them in the dark," she said.

"You can sit next to me, Dawn," said Poppy.

The little girl settled down beside Poppy. "This is my very first slumber party," she said proudly.

Sue was turning off the lamps.

"All of the lights?" Jane Ellen sounded nervous.

"All," said Tink.

Maria snapped off the small lamp on the TV set.

A soft glow came from the hall. "Why don't we leave that one on?" asked Jane Ellen.

"Out!" Tink said sternly. "I tell my best spookies in the dark."

10
The Spooky

With the streetlights painting tree shadows on the walls, the room seemed strange and mysterious. Everyone crowded around Tink and she began.

"Listen, my dears, and you shall hear"—she made her voice deep and said the words slowly, importantly—"the tale of what once happened in this . . . very . . . house."

The room was still.

She made her voice softer. Everyone leaned forward to hear better.

"Because of what once happened here, the ghost of a girl has been seen in this house. She's no older than us. She wears a white nightgown that's dirty, marked with soot from the—" She stopped. She didn't want to tell that part yet. She had to tell the story slowly, so the sounds would come at the right times. "And people have heard her moan."

She touched the button on the tape recorder.

Nobody heard the click. But everyone heard the soft moan that whispered through the room.

Maria giggled. "You tell the best spookies, Tink."

"Silence," said Tink in her deepest story-telling voice. "Once long ago a really super-rich salesman—no, I mean merchant—lived here with his glamorous wife and pretty little daughter. They lived in the whole house, not just in one of the apartments. The lady was as beautiful as. . .as. . .Cinderella at the ball. And the little girl was as. . .as dainty as a fairy princess.

"They wore clothes of pink velvet trimmed with gold. They never wore the same clothes twice— they just gave them to the servants. They laughed a lot. And they had fancy balls—that's what they used to call parties in the olden days—in the ballroom up on the top floor."

"The Kenneseys live there now," said Erin. "It's a studio apartment."

"I must have silence," Tink said sternly.

There were giggles.

Tink waited. When everyone was quiet again, she continued.

"Then one terrible, horrible dark night, robbers came." She touched the tape recorder. The creaking sound of a door slowly opening filled the room.

Someone gasped. It sounded like Jane Ellen.

Heads turned to look at the living room door. Nothing was there.

"The robbers came in," Tink went on. "They piled all the silver and gold and rubies and diamonds and pearls in a heap in the downstairs hall."

A loud clanking and rattle came from the tape.

"Then they went to the bedroom — I mean bed chamber — of the master and mistress of this very house. They murdered them in their beds. The blood and gore was something awful."

Someone said "OOOoooo," softly.

"The robbers trampled the blood all over this very house. Because, you see, they were looking for the little girl. Only they couldn't find her because she had climbed up inside the fireplace chimney downstairs in the living room. Her teeth were clacking together—"

Was that the sound of chattering teeth everyone heard?

"And she was sighing, 'Oh, my papa. Oh, my

mama. Where are you?' That's what kids called their parents in those days.

"Well, the robbers couldn't find her, and they didn't hear her teeth clacking and her pitiful sad sighs. So they stuffed the silver and gold and precious jewels into sacks and went away."

A door creaked shut.

"After the robbers were gone, the little girl followed the bloody footsteps to her parents' bed chamber. When she saw them she gave out this terrible shriek and died on the spot."

Someone in the room giggled nervously.

"The next day," Tink went on, "the police came. They found the little girl. Her white nightgown was covered with black soot. And this is the really horrible thing: her...hair...had... turned...snow...white! But it didn't matter, of course, because she was dead anyway.

"And ever since that day, every now and then, people in this house hear moaning. Sometimes they even hear shrieking."

She touched the button on the tape recorder. The soft moan sighed through the room again. But this time it was followed by blood-curdling screams.

The screams went on and on—even after Tink turned off the tape recorder.

The overhead lights flashed on. Mrs. Lawson rushed into the room. She scooped up the screaming Dawn and sat down, rocking back and forth.

"There, there," she crooned. "What frightened mother's girl? There, now."

"There's a ghost here," wailed Dawn. "People see it—and it—screams." She began screaming again, only this time her shrieks were muffled against her mother's shoulder.

"Now, now," Mrs. Lawson said soothingly, "there are no ghosts in this house. Even if there were, would Mother let her girl see one?"

Dawn's screams turned to sobs. Mrs. Lawson kept rocking her.

All Tink could see were the words *I'm Cute* on the back of Dawn's pajamas. But for some reason those words gave her that maybe-I'm-going-to-throw-up feeling she always got when she was in trouble.

Mrs. Lawson looked around at the girls. "What's been going on here?"

The girls looked at each other uncomfortably.

"Just a spooky," said Erin. "A ghost story."

"It was fun," said Lisa.

"Who told this fun ghost story?" asked Mrs. Lawson.

"I did," said Tink. She wished she were somewhere else. Anywhere else.

At the sound of Tink's voice, Dawn's wails rose again.

Mrs. Lawson gave her a little shake and a hug. "Mother's girl is perfectly safe. Now"—she looked from face to face—"can we all think of happy things? I'll start. The park on a sunny day."

"Pigeons," said Poppy.

"Ice-cream cones," said Maria.

"Boys on bikes," said Lisa.

Feeling a little silly, everyone said the happiest things they could think of. Flowers...the play lot...joggers...wading in the pond....

"Blue sky and clouds," said Mrs. Lawson. She put a finger under Dawn's chin and tipped up her face. "What can mother's girl think of?"

Dawn had stopped crying. Her lower lip stuck out. "Rain," she said.

And that was the last game at Erin's party.

"I'll talk to you later, Erin," said Mrs. Lawson. "And to you, Tink. There are to be no more ghost stories tonight."

Erin's birthday cake was a pizza—made of ice cream! The candles sat around the edge.

"It was my idea," Erin said happily. "Only I didn't make it—my mom did. Can you guess what's in it?" She didn't wait for an answer. "The crust is French Vanilla. The cheese is pumpkin. The little pieces that look like meat are chocolate. And the tomato sauce is pink because it's strawberry. Of course," she added, "we can't pick it up like real pizza. We'll have to eat it with spoons."

Nobody minded eating the "pizza" with spoons. Not the least bit.

Afterward, Erin opened her presents. She got some pink notepaper and pink sealing wax and a stamp with an *E* for Erin. There was a T-shirt with the words *I'm So Confused* on the back. There was a denim purse with Erin's name in patchwork that Poppy's mother had made. There were silly stickers for Erin's collection. But she seemed to like Tink's present best—a pen with a light in it so she could write in the dark.

They all opened their sleeping bags and talked and watched TV as long as they could stay awake. But they didn't stay awake all night. At last the sound of sleepy breathing filled the room.

"Tink?" Poppy whispered.

"What?" Tink whispered back.

"Know something?" whispered Poppy. "Mrs. Lawson talks in questions—just the way Erin always does!"

It was true! Nearly everything Mrs. Lawson said *did* come out a question!

Tink and Poppy buried their mouths in their sleeping bags and giggled.

Tink came awake with a jump. Someone was trying to pry open her eyes!

She opened them herself.

Sunlight filled the room. Dawn was kneeling next to her.

Tink raised up onto her elbows. Everyone was still asleep.

"Tink," whispered Dawn. "What's a ghost?"

11

"Pea Soup for Brains"

"But where did you get all the rattling and creaking and screaming noises?" asked Tink's mother the evening after the slumber party. That was after Mrs. Lawson called and told her about the spooky.

"Got some of them from that old record of spooky sound effects," said Tink. "Put them on my tape recorder. And I made up some — I'm a pretty good screamer. I practiced and practiced to get the creaks and rattles in the right places."

Her mother shook her head. "I know you girls like scary stories. I did, too, when I was your age, but you didn't use common sense. Erin's sister is too little for such stuff."

"Mrs. Lawson scolded me," said Tink. "And she scolded Erin, too. That wasn't fair, because it was all my fault." Tink wasn't one bit happy with herself. "I get into such — such tangles! And the spooky was a good idea. Everyone wanted to hear it."

Her mother rinsed their soup bowls. She laughed. "I'm almost ready to believe what you say about red hair and trouble."

Tink perked up. "You are? Then will you—"

"No," said her mother. "I will not color your hair. Someday you're going to like your red hair."

"Ha!" said Tink.

School went smoothly. Mrs. Kincaid was nice. She didn't mind when everyone laughed. When the class got too loud she would call, "All right, everyone, let's cut it down to a quiet roar."

One day during language arts she talked about plural and singular. "Some words are the same whether you mean one or many of a thing. For example—*sheep*. You can have one sheep or many."

"Fish," said Poppy. "It can mean one or lots."

"Pants," said Brian. "I never heard of anyone wearing a pant."

"Scissors," said Sue. "Nobody says they have lots of scissorses."

Tink thought of one. "Hair," she said, looking right at Sue. "Nobody says 'Make my hairs look gorgeous.' "

96

Poppy, Lisa, Maria, Erin, and Jane Ellen burst into giggles. They remembered Tink's House of Gorgeousness.

Mrs. Kincaid looked puzzled. "I don't get that joke," she said, "but if you all want a good laugh, well, I say it's wholesome for the liver."

Mrs. Kincaid had a funny way of saying things.

One day when she was helping her mother dust, Tink came across that funny old book—*Mrs. Ione Tuttleby's Hints for Happiness*.

She stopped dusting and stood reading. It was as interesting as the first time she saw it. Suddenly she had an idea!

Then, "Trouble," she thought. "Will I get into trouble?" But—how could she get into trouble with such a good idea? Mrs. Tuttleby's book was going to help make everyone happy.

She forgot about dusting. She ran to the phone and called Poppy.

Poppy's brother Wilding answered. "City Zoo. We are open from nine to four. Animal feedings are—"

"Wilding! It's me, Wilding," said Tink. "I want to talk to—"

Wilding went right on talking. "—at eleven and four-thirty—"

"Wilding!" yelled Tink. "Is Poppy there?"

"I'm sorry," said Wilding in a grown-up voice. "Animals are not allowed to come to the phone. But if you would care to—"

"Wilding!" screamed Tink, "I'm going to come over there and—"

"Hey, Tink, hi," Wilding said mildly. "Are you upset about something? I'll bet you want to talk to Poppy. Just a min—"

Tink groaned. She heard the phone drop. Sounds came over the line. The TV. Footsteps. A little voice said, "Hi, this is Daisy," and giggled and didn't wait for an answer. Nilly meowed.

When Tink thought she couldn't stand it anymore, Poppy answered.

"Popp! I've got the greatest idea," said Tink. "I mean, a really good one. And it won't get anyone in trouble. Can you come over? Bring Sue and Lisa. I'll call Maria."

"Jane Ellen, too?" asked Poppy.

"Uh—" Tink made a face. "I suppose so."

"She'll cry if we leave her out," said Poppy.

Tink sighed. "She's sort of trying to be better."

"I'll tell her, too," said Poppy.

Tink hung up and called Maria. Then she ran downstairs, hugging the book. She practiced jumping from the top step until everyone got there. When they did, she started talking before they had a chance to sit down.

"Just listen," she said. "It says in this book by a lady named Mrs. Tuttleby"—she held it up—"there's a way to make yourself happy."

Tink opened the book and began reading. "'Gather the happy things of life around yourselves, my dears. You will be dipping into—the Sugarbowl of Life.'"

"Why does she call us 'my dears?'" asked Erin. "She doesn't know us."

"This is a really old book," said Tink. "That's how people used to talk. Here's how it works. Erin, you're always asking questions. In the *Q* part Mrs. Tuttleby says, 'To ask questions means you will always seek the truth.' So now you know about your future."

"Maybe I'll be a private eye when I grow up," said Erin.

"But don't you see?" asked Tink. "Why can't we look up the things we wish would happen to us and then do whatever Mrs. Tuttleby says we have to do to make them happen?"

Maria got the idea. "Like, if I wanted to be a private eye, I could start asking questions?"

"Right!" Tink just loved her new idea! "Mrs. Tuttleby says, 'To see candy means you will have sweet dreams.' So why don't we go look at candy and have sweet dreams tonight?"

"So if you wanted to be popular," said Jane Ellen, "you'd just do whatever Mrs. Tuttleby says and then it would happen to you?" She looked dreamy.

"Right," said Tink.

"If you wanted to go to a party—" said Lisa.

"—you'd do the things Mrs. Tuttleby says lead up to a party," finished Erin.

"Know what I think?" asked Sue. "I think that book is dumb-o. What is, *is*. I don't think you can use tricks to make things like that happen."

"But why not try?" said Tink. "Let's test it. Let's each look at the book and pick out one thing we want. Then we'll do whatever Mrs. Tuttleby says

100

we have to do to get it. Tomorrow after school we'll meet again and tell what our wishes were and if they came true."

Lisa's eyes danced. "I know what I want." She reached for the book. "Let me see if Mrs. Tuttleby says how to get it."

The girls crowded around her, reading, looking for the special things each one wanted. As soon as they found what they were looking for, they went home. At last only Tink and Poppy were left.

Poppy studied the book for a long time. At last she smiled and closed it.

"Do you know what you want?" asked Tink.

"You bet," said Poppy. "I guess we can't go looking together, though."

Tink agreed. "Not if we're really testing the book."

She watched Poppy go off down Greenbrier Street. When Poppy came to a fire hydrant, she leap-frogged over it.

"I know what I want most of all," thought Tink, pushing her hair back from her face. And Mrs. Tuttleby's book was going to make her wish come true.

Tink had a pocket radio. She carried it to school with her the next morning. She knew what she was going to do.

After math, while everyone was reading, Tink asked to go to the restroom.

Mrs. Kincaid said yes. "But don't dawdle. Come straight back."

Tink closed the door softly. The hall was empty.

She hurried downstairs. Nobody was in the hall there, either.

She was really lucky. She wasn't even going to have to borrow a broom from Mr. Swenson's cleaning closet. She had seen one just that morning in the first-floor hall.

She thought of the words in Mrs. Tuttleby's book.

> To dance with a broom is a sign of a speedy improvement in your life.

She wasn't going to dance with any old broom, not the kind her mother used to sweep the kitchen. She needed a big improvement in her life, and she wanted the biggest broom in the world—the kind Mr. Swenson used.

She skidded to a stop. There it was, where she

had seen it, across the doorway of an empty classroom.

She snapped on her pocket radio, softly, and grabbed the broom. She turned it so the brush was at the top. The broom was tippy, upside down, and she held it carefully. Then she danced into the room doing a rock step she had seen on TV.

She was halfway across the floor before she felt the stickiness under her feet.

She stopped and looked down. Something was wrong with the floor.

"What are you doing in my room, girl?" boomed a voice from the door. Mr. Swenson stood there, glaring at her.

A sick feeling settled in Tink's stomach. "Dancing, Mr. Swenson," she said. Her voice shook.

"I think you have got pea soup for brains, that's what I think." Mr. Swenson's eyes gave off sparks. "Yah! Pea soup. Didn't you see the broom in the doorway? Look." He pointed.

Tink looked. Her footprints made a trail across the floor. They led from the door straight to where she stood.

"You have ruined my floor," said Mr. Swenson.

"Come with me. We go and see Mr. Tippitt. We ask him why you have pea soup for brains."

Tink tiptoed with noisy, sticky-sounding steps to the door. Mr. Swenson took the broom and leaned it across the doorway again.

He led the way down the hall. "Pea soup! Such a girl! Such music!" He turned to her. "Make out that music," he said sternly.

Tink turned off her pocket radio. She followed Mr. Swenson into the principal's office.

12
Do Wishes Come True?

"Well, Melissa," said Mr. Tippitt, "I hoped I wouldn't be seeing as much of you this year as I did last."

Tink wanted to die.

Mr. Tippitt turned to Mr. Swenson and heard all that he had to say. At last Mr. Swenson ran out of words and went grumbling back to his work.

Mr. Tippitt leaned back in his chair. He made a tent of his fingers. "Why are you in school, Melissa?"

"To study and learn things," whispered Tink.

"Mm-mmm," said Mr. Tippitt. "Now, can you tell me why you were dancing with a broom in an empty classroom? When you were supposed to be in your own classroom? Learning everything Mrs. Kincaid can teach you?"

Suddenly Tink didn't want to tell him why she was dancing. Suddenly it all sounded silly.

"I'm waiting, Melissa," said Mr. Tippitt. "I'm sure this is going to be an unusual story."

So Tink had to tell him about the book and about how it was supposed to help her to get a special wish.

"Perhaps you'd like to tell me about this special wish, Melissa," said Mr. Tippitt. His voice was kind.

Tink told him. About the awfulness of red hair. About red hair being a jinx. "Even my really good, best ideas get me into trouble," she said. "I know it's because of my hair."

"Mm-mm," said Mr. Tippitt. He looked thoughtful. "I really don't think red hair is a jinx—that it causes your troubles. Let me think some more about that. But in the meantime, perhaps you'd like to share the name of this remarkable book with me. It sounds like one we all could use."

Tink looked at the floor. *"Mrs. Ione Tuttleby's Hints for Happiness,"* she said, *"or, How to Dip into the Sugarbowl of Life."*

Mr. Tippitt's voice shook slightly. "I would like to see this astonishing book, Melissa," he said.

Tink looked up at him. Was Mr. Tippitt laughing? No. She could see that he wasn't.

"You have caused Mr. Swenson a great deal of extra work," said Mr. Tippitt. "You were in the halls without permission, doing something you weren't supposed to do. I'm sure Mrs. Kincaid didn't know what you were up to. Today you are to do your work at the detention desk in the outer office. Mrs. Kincaid will bring your lessons to you."

He went on. "I think your mother and I should have a talk."

Things were as bad as they had ever been in Tink's whole life!

The rest of the day she worked at a desk near the door. And every time someone went past, she knew they were wondering what kind of terrible kid she was. She wanted to hide under the desk.

The girls—all but Lisa—were waiting on the steps when she got home.

"Did Mr. Tippitt scold you for something?" asked Poppy.

Tink made a face. "Mr. Tippitt scolded. Mr. Swenson scolded. Mrs. Kincaid scolded. When my mom comes home, I'll be scolded some more."

"Poor Tink," Poppy said softly.

"But what did you *do*?" asked Sue. "Was it something about your wish?"

"I didn't see how looking for happy things could get me into trouble." Tink sighed. "But this is the worst tangle I've ever been in.

"Mrs. Tuttleby's book said 'To dance with a broom is a sign of speedy improvement in your life.' Well, getting rid of this red hair would be an improvement. Red hair causes all my bad luck. I want my mom to color it."

"Bleach it?" asked Maria, her eyes round.

"They do it to kid TV stars all the time," said Tink.

"Why would dancing with a broom make anyone's life better?" wondered Sue.

"Anyway," said Tink, "there was this broom, Mr. Swenson's broom—"

The girls groaned.

"—in front of the doorway of this empty room," said Tink. And she told what had happened.

"Even though Mr. Tippitt scolded you," said Maria, "you did what the book said. So maybe your wish will come true after all."

Yesterday afternoon and their plans seemed like a million years ago. Tink looked around at her friends. "Did you all get your wishes?"

"I didn't," said Sue. "The book said 'To ride a bicycle uphill is to know that your dearest wish will come true.' So I found this bike, unlocked, against the tree in front of your house, Poppy."

"Oh, no!" said Poppy. "Fielding's bike!"

"I rode it uphill," Sue went on. "It's sort of uphill in front of your house."

"It's hardly uphill at all," said Poppy.

"But it's not really flat," said Sue. "Anyway, Fielding came running after me. I didn't get to ride far, and I fell off because it's such a big bike. Now there's a scratch on the fender. Ohhhh, Fielding was mad."

"What was your dearest wish?" asked Erin.

"My wish," said Sue, "is to be bat girl for the Cubs."

"Wow!" said Tink. "You don't pick 'em small!"

"Well, I didn't believe that dumb-o book anyway," said Sue. "So why not make my wish a big one?"

"My wish was smaller," said Jane Ellen. "But I

guess it won't come true because I couldn't find a nutmeg."

"A what?" asked Poppy.

"Mrs. Tuttleby said, 'To warm a whole nutmeg in your hands until it gives off its scent is a sign of friendship forever true,'" said Jane Ellen, looking at Tink. "So I went looking for a whole nutmeg. My mom said she only has them during the holidays. I asked everyone I knew, but nobody had a whole nutmeg."

She sniffed the palms of her hands. "I rubbed some of the powdery kind on my hands, but I don't think that's going to make my wish come true."

She looked sadly at Tink.

Tink was relieved. She thought she knew what Jane Ellen's wish was. Jane Ellen wanted to be her best friend. Tink was glad Jane Ellen hadn't found a nutmeg. She also felt sad. And bad. Why didn't she want Jane Ellen for a best friend?

Poppy spoke up. "Mrs. Tuttleby said that to hurtle—that means to jump over—many things is a sure sign that you will succeed in everything you try. Well, I'd like to succeed in keeping the twins out of trouble when I'm babysitting for them.

"I jumped over a fence," she said, "and over the bars in front of Columbo's in-out doors. I jumped over six trash cans in the alley. Tomorrow I have to take care of the twins after school. I'll see if all that jumping worked."

"I was supposed to eat jam while sitting in the sunlight," said Erin. "It meant I would go on a journey. I wanted my dad to take us to the Museum of Science and Industry.

"So I got a jar of strawberry jam out of the fridge, and I sat downstairs on the back steps. I ate it with a spoon, without bread or anything. The jam was really good, only it made my tooth hurt. Then my mom came downstairs and saw me holding my face. She looked in my mouth. Then she went and called the dentist. My journey is going to be to the dentist!"

"Oh-h-h-h," they all sighed.

"What I was supposed to do," said Maria, "was to touch a crown—"

"A crown!" said Tink. "But we don't have kings in this country. How could you touch a crown?"

Maria looked smug. "Well, I knew where there was a crown. There's a store on Clark Street that rents clothes for weddings and fancy parties. In the window, there's a crown like Miss America wears. I went in there and asked if I could touch it. They let me."

"What happened?" asked Erin. "Wow! A crown."

"Mrs. Tuttleby's book said if I touched a crown my fortunes would rise. I want my mother to let *me* rise—to let *me* grow *up*," said Maria. "Well, afterward I went home. My mom had been shopping. She bought me a dress."

"But that's good," said Tink.

"That's bad!" Maria looked sour. "That dress has little yellow ducks all across the front of it. Baby old ducks!"

The girls groaned.

Lisa was coming up Greenbrier Street. They waved to her.

"Hurry up, Lees," called Tink. "Maybe something good happened to Lisa," she said.

Lisa looked glum.

"What happened?" asked Erin.

Lisa plopped down on the steps. "Mrs. Tuttleby's book said that daisies don't lie. And I wanted to know if Timmy O'Brien likes me. Do you know about taking the petals off daisies?" she asked, looking around.

"He loves me, he loves me not," said Maria.

"Yes," said Lisa. "I went to Columbo's flower counter after school. They always have flowers standing around in buckets of water. Well, I just took some petals off one daisy, saying, 'He loves me, he loves me not.' I didn't even take the daisy out of the bucket."

"You did that right there in the store?" asked Erin.

"Uh-huh," said Lisa. "Then the manager walked by. He grabbed my arm. He asked my name. He said he would call my mother. And he said he was going to call Armbruster, too." Her voice shook.

"Oh, my," sighed Poppy.

"But the worst part of it," wailed Lisa, "was—I ended on 'He loves me not'!"

13

A Really Awful Kid

Tink and her mother were sitting on the sofa watching TV. Her mother was filing her nails. Tink had already had her scolding, so that was over. But she felt worse than she had ever felt in her whole life. She felt lonesome. But how could that be? Her mother was right there beside her.

Tomorrow they had to see Mr. Tippitt.

And Mrs. Kincaid was probably thinking awful thoughts about her.

Erin had to go to the dentist. Maria had to wear a dress with ducks on it. Jane Ellen wasn't going to be her best friend, and Tink felt mean for being glad. Worst of all, Lisa was in trouble, too.

It was all her fault. Every single horrible thing was her fault.

"Mom?" she asked. "Would you rock me?"

"Rock you!" said her mother. "A big kid like you? And anyway—we haven't got a rocking chair."

"If we did have a rocking chair," asked Tink, "would you rock me?"

Her mother gave a last scrape to her fingernail and dropped the file. "Honestly, sometimes you're a real stitch! Asking to be rocked when we haven't got a rocking chair! What's getting into you?"

Tink tugged at a loose thread on the sofa. "Sometimes when Poppy feels bad, her mother rocks her. She told me. Pretty soon she feels better."

Her mother reached out and pulled her close. "I can't rock you, but I guess I can give you a great big hug."

Tink liked that.

"And I guess I can tickle you," said her mother, doing just that.

"No," shrieked Tink, laughing and squirming, trying to get away. "I'll die if you don't stop," she gasped. "I'll die."

Her mother was laughing, too. She stopped the tickling, but she kept her arm around Tink.

It felt strange and nice to sit with her mother's arm around her. Strange because they weren't very huggy people, but nice because it was cozy.

116

"Scared about tomorrow?" asked her mother.

Tink nodded.

"Well, Punkin, you've got to face the music," said her mother. "Nothing so terrible can happen. I mean, I'll be there."

"Everyone thinks I'm a really awful kid," said Tink.

Her mother mussed her hair. "I don't think you're so awful. And Poppy and your other friends don't seem to think so, either."

"Mr. Tippitt does. And I'll bet Mrs. Kincaid thinks I'm going to be in trouble all this school year. And I'll bet Lisa's mom is mad at me. And—"

"I'll bet someday you're going to laugh about this," said her mother.

Tink shook her head. "Never."

"You'll see," said her mother.

"Do you really think so?" asked Tink.

"Know so," said her mother.

Tink remembered something else. "Jane Ellen wants to be best friends with me. Only I don't want to be best friends with her."

"That's a sticky problem," said her mother.

"I feel so mean," said Tink.

Her mother thought about that for a while, staring at the TV, biting her lip. At last she turned to Tink. "Well, the way I figure things, you don't have to like everyone, but you've got to be nice to everyone. You don't have to be best friends with Jane Ellen. But you can't be mean to her."

"But how nice do I have to be?" asked Tink. "Do I have to walk to school with her every day? Or stand next to her in line in gym? Or go to her house instead of Poppy's after school?"

Her mother shook her head. "No, to all of those. What I mean is, you can't make fun of her, or. . . be unfair to her."

"Of course, she is trying to be nicer lately," said Tink. "Everyone says so. She doesn't push ahead of everyone in line anymore. Sometimes she shares her candy. But she still says mean things when she gets mad. When TJ wouldn't let her use his orange felt-tip pen she called him 'fatso.' She said his cheeks jiggle when he runs."

"That was mean," agreed her mother. "No wonder she has trouble making friends. Well, just remember there's safety in numbers. When Jane

Ellen wants you all to herself, ask the other girls to play, too. Include her in. One of these days when she's nice to everyone all of the time, she'll find a best friend."

"I sure hope so," said Tink.

"Know so," said her mother.

Tink's mind bounced back to her other troubles. "If I can just live through tomorrow..." she sighed. She thought again of being rocked. "When I was a baby, did you rock me?"

Her mother shook her head. "Not even then. You were a little wiggler. And you had a cute laugh. That's why I started calling you Tinkerbell. But do you know what I did do when you fussed?"

"What?"

"I danced with you in my arms and you always settled down and went to sleep."

"Did you really?" asked Tink. She couldn't think of herself as small enough to fit in her mother's arms. "Did I have red hair even then?"

"Even then," said her mother. "And do you know something else? Sometimes your dad and I would dance with you between us. We were practically babies ourselves! We were only seventeen!"

119

"Did they have rock music in those days?" asked Tink.

"Yes. But you won't believe this," said her mother. "What you liked was waltzing. We'd waltz around the room—*one*-two-three. . .*one*-two-three—to soft music. Soon you'd be snoring."

"I don't snore!" said Tink. She was outraged.

"Did then. Do now," said her mother.

"Don't," said Tink.

"Do," said her mother. "Now that I think of it—"

She got up, turned off the TV, and knelt in front of the record cabinet. She pulled out records until she found the one she was looking for. "Here. Listen to this," she said.

She put it on the turntable they hardly ever used anymore. Now they listened mostly to tapes. "Come here," said her mother.

Tink went to stand in front of her mother.

Lilting music filled the room.

"Can you hear the beat?" asked her mother. "It goes *one*-two-three. . .*step*-step-step. . .*step*-step-step." She put her arm around Tink's shoulders and took her right hand.

And Tink and her mother waltzed around and around the room. For a while, Tink forgot about being a really awful kid.

14
Mr. Dragon

The school office seemed awfully crowded. Mrs. Owens and Lisa were there when Tink and her mother arrived. Tink carried Mrs. Tuttleby's book. She liked the feel of it in her hands. Maybe it was a silly book—but it was fun all the same.

Mrs. Owens just looked at Tink. Her eyes were like blue icicles. But she said hello quite nicely to Tink's mother.

Lisa lifted a hand shyly. She smiled, a scared smile.

Lisa and Mrs. Owens went into Mr. Tippitt's office first. After a while Lisa came out alone. Her mother stayed with Mr. Tippitt.

"Was it bad?" whispered Tink.

"Know what I have to do?" whispered Lisa. "I have to use my savings to pay for the daisies—the whole bunch—when I only touched one flower. And I won't get any spending money for two weeks, either."

"That's terrible," whispered Tink. "You won't be able to buy candy or anything."

Lisa looked sad. Then she began to smile. "But if the whole bunch is mine, I can take all the petals off. Maybe the very last one will be 'He loves me.'"

Tink didn't have time to say anything. Mrs. Owens was coming out of Mr. Tippitt's office. She came straight to Tink. "Tink," she said, "kindly promise not to lead Lisa into trouble again."

"Oh, I promise, Mrs. Owens," said Tink. "Cross my heart."

Then it was her turn. She followed her mother into Mr. Tippitt's office.

Mr. Tippitt shook hands with her mother. "It's good to see you, Mrs. Becker. This is the first time this year, isn't it? It's too bad our meetings always seem to be stress filled."

Tink felt her mother's arm go around her shoulders.

Mr. Tippitt looked down at Tink. "I've been thinking about your red hair, Melissa, and I don't agree that it's a jinx."

"I wish you could make her believe that," said Tink's mother. "I can't."

"A lot of famous people have red hair," said Mr. Tippitt. "Did you know that Thomas Jefferson had red hair? He wrote the Declaration of Independence. And he became president. Now that doesn't sound like he was jinxed, does it?"

Tink had to agree. If someone with red hair got to be president, maybe red hair wasn't a jinx.

Mr. Tippitt went on. "I've talked about this with Mrs. Kincaid, and she's going to work with you on a special project. I think it will prove something to you. You are going to find out about all the famous people in history who had red hair."

"All of them?" gasped Tink.

Mr. Tippitt laughed. "You might end up liking the project. You might even become famous for knowing more than anybody about all the redheads in history."

Tink giggled.

"No," said Mr. Tippitt, "your red hair isn't at the bottom of your problems. Now, tell me, do you have any plan for staying out of trouble?"

Tink took a deep breath. She had thought about that a lot last night. "I can *not* have any more good ideas," she said. She added, "Only I don't know how to do that."

Mr. Tippitt looked thoughtful. "Melissa," he said, "that's not the answer. I don't want you to stop having good ideas."

Tink's mouth dropped open. "You don't? But my good ideas always turn into trouble."

"There are too few good ideas in this world," said Mr. Tippitt. "We can't afford to ignore them. No, don't give up on your good ideas."

Tink felt dizzy. If her red hair didn't cause her to get into trouble. . . and if she wasn't supposed to stop having good ideas. . . what could she do? Mr. Tippitt even wanted her to keep on having good ideas. She was confused. "But," she said, "but—"

"Somehow," said Mr. Tippitt, "you must learn to think things through. That's where your problem lies."

"That's what I've been telling her," said Tink's mother.

"Will you work on thinking things through, Melissa?" asked Mr. Tippitt.

Tink nodded.

"And I suppose," said Mr. Tippitt, "you'd like to tell Mr. Swenson you're sorry for the extra work you've caused him."

Tink drew a circle on the floor with the toe of her shoe. "I can tell him I'll never dance with a broom in school again," she whispered.

"Good idea," said Mr. Tippitt. "Mr. Swenson works hard to keep Armbruster ship-shape. He'll be glad to know you won't be attacking the school with a broom again."

Tink remembered something else. "I brought you Mrs. Tuttleby's book," she said, "not just to look at, but for you to keep. It's lots of fun." She put the book on his desk. How she hated to give it up! "I really don't want to get Lisa or anyone in trouble again."

"You've made a wise decision, Melissa," said Mr. Tippitt. "I'm certain I'll enjoy reading Mrs. Tuttleby's book. Now suppose you wait outside. I'd like to talk with your mother."

So Tink sat in the outer office again. She wondered what Mr. Tippitt and her mother were talking about. She leaned toward the closed door. She thought she heard something. Was it laughter? Were Mr. Tippitt and her mother laughing?

No! That couldn't be! She was in trouble. Her

mother and Mr. Tippitt wouldn't laugh.

It was a long time before her mother came out. "Okay, Punkin," she said. "Let's go."

"You mean out of school? You mean not go to my classroom?"

"First," said her mother, "we're going to find Mr. Swenson. You have something to say to him. Then you and I are taking the morning off. You'll come back to school later. Now, where's Mr. Dragon-Swenson?"

They found Mr. Swenson on the second floor. Tools lay all around him. He was fixing the drinking fountain.

"So that's Mr. Dragon," whispered her mother. "Funny—he just looks like an old man, to me. As a matter of fact, with that droopy mustache, he looks like a nice old walrus."

Tink giggled. She felt shy as they went toward Mr. Swenson.

Mr. Swenson sat back on his heels. "Yah," he said. "So it's you, is it?"

Tink gulped. "I'm really glad you keep our school ship-shape, Mr. Swenson," she said. "I'm sorry I messed up your floor. I didn't think ahead."

"Will you do that again?" asked Mr. Swenson.

"Never," promised Tink. "Honest, I won't."

Mr. Swenson looked up at her mother.

"Oh," said Tink. "This is my mom."

Her mother smiled at him. And Mr. Swenson smiled back! He got to his feet, and he touched his forehead as though he was wearing a hat and was tipping it.

"How are you, lady?" asked Mr. Swenson.

Tink stared from Mr. Swenson to her mother. People always smiled at her mother. But who would think Mr. Swenson would smile! It was the first time she had ever seen him smile at anybody.

"My daughter has promised to think before she acts from now on," said her mother. "Is there any way I can help fix up that floor?"

"Oh—no, no, no," said Mr. Swenson. "Is a strong man's job. Is almost fixed."

"Well, I'm glad about that. And thank you for being so nice about it," said her mother. She took Tink's hand and they went to the stairway.

Tink looked back. Mr. Swenson was still standing, his tools around his feet. He was looking after them. And he was still smiling.

15
One Smart Kid

"But why are you taking the whole morning off from work?" asked Tink.

They were sitting in a booth at the Golden Nugget Pancake House. Tink was eating pancakes and raspberry syrup, because she had been too upset to eat breakfast that morning. Her mother was drinking coffee.

"I took the whole morning off," said her mother, "because I didn't know how long Mr. Tippitt and I would have to talk."

Tink looked up from her pancakes. "You were laughing with Mr. Tippitt," she said. "I heard you."

"Laughing?" said her mother. "Are you *sure* you heard laughing? Because we were having a very serious talk about you."

Then Tink wasn't sure she had heard laughing.

"What did Mr. Tippitt say about me?"

Her mother sipped her coffee. "He called you a natural leader."

"What does that mean?" asked Tink.

"It means people like to do the things you do."

Tink waited for more.

"And we talked about those good ideas of yours."

Tink poured more raspberry syrup on her pancakes.

"Hey! Let me have a bite," said her mother, "just one bite." She took Tink's fork and ate a piece of pancake. "Yummy! Well, I hope you'll begin to understand soon that having red hair doesn't cause your troubles. And I hope you'll learn to think about what might happen before you act on those good ideas of yours."

"It sure is hard to guess what might happen when you have an idea," said Tink.

"You just need more practice," said her mother. "If you really can't figure things out, you can always touch base with me.

"That Mr. Tippitt's one smart man," she went on. "He thinks your ideas are creative. He said you have enough imagination and energy for three kids." She rested her head on her hand. "I'm glad I've got just one of you to cope with."

Tink's heart flip-flopped. "Would you be glad not to have me at all? Then you could go out nights, and nobody would fuss, and—"

"Dumbo!" Her mother laughed. "What would I do without you? There wouldn't be anyone to eat up all the green Popsicles and try on my jewelry."

Tink giggled and felt better. Then she remembered why she was at the Golden Nugget instead of in school. "I guess I still have to apologize to Mrs. Kincaid," she said. What a horrible idea!

"Well, I just guess!" said her mother.

"Did Mr. Tippitt say anything else?" asked Tink.

"Yes. He had another idea, and I had one too."

Tink wasn't sure she liked both her mother and Mr. Tippitt having ideas about her. She looked at her mother suspiciously.

"Eat up, before your food gets cold." Her mother set down her cup. "We talked about how much you like telling your spookies—"

"Why did you tell him about that?" moaned Tink.

"He was giving out good advice," said her mother, "and I thought we could use some. Anyway, if Mrs. Kincaid says okay, and if Mrs. Morgan the librarian agrees, you're going to help with story hour for the first grades once a week."

Tink's eyes sparkled. "Really? But"—her forehead wrinkled—"that sounds like fun, not punishment."

"It sounds to Mr. Tippitt like learning how to make the most of your talents," said her mother. "You like to tell stories—maybe you'll learn how to do it better." She picked up her purse. "Finished?"

She left a tip for the waitress and paid for their breakfast at the counter. Tink poked her arms into her jacket. She ran after her mother. "Where are we going?" she asked. "And what was your idea?"

"You'll see," said her mother. "Now hurry. Our bus is coming."

The bus ride seemed long to Tink. "Where is this bus going?" she asked.

"To the end of the line," said her mother. "That's where buses go."

"You're doing it to me again," said Tink.

"Doing what?"

"Taking me someplace and not telling me where," said Tink. "Give me a hint," she begged.

"Okay," said her mother. "One hint. You need energy for this."

Tink thought about that for a while. "I can't guess," she said.

"Good," said her mother. And that's all she would say.

After a while her mother said, "Next block."

Tink pulled the cord and the bus stopped. They got off, walked a half block, and stopped in front of a door.

Tink read the sign on the door. "Madame Popova's School of the Dance."

"I'm going to sign you up for dancing class," said her mother. "You're going to come here and use up some of that extra energy of yours."

Tink was excited. She loved to dance. "Will I learn to tap dance?" she asked as they went inside and climbed to the second floor.

"I'd like you to take ballet," said her mother.

Tink remembered ballet dancers she had seen on TV. They looked like butterflies. They floated. They danced on the tips of their toes. She couldn't believe this was all really happening to her.

"You'll learn to be graceful, even if you don't learn anything else," said her mother. "And I'll know what you're up to after school—at least some of the time."

While her mother talked to a woman at a desk, Tink looked around. Two older girls in black tights crossed the hall and went into a room. Piano music came from another room. Tink peeked inside.

The room was big. One wall was covered with a mirror. A long rail was fastened to the opposite wall.

A dozen very little girls and boys were in the room. They were trying to dance. Their teacher was showing them how to point their toes and how to hold their arms above their heads.

The children turned and stared at Tink.

The teacher glanced toward the door. She shook her head. Tink closed the door. Her toes itched to dance to the music.

"—at four on Tuesday and another class on Saturday morning," the desk lady was saying.

"Expect her both days, then," said Tink's mother. "She'll be coming alone, so you'll have to show her what she's supposed to do at first."

"I'm Miss Grainger," said the desk lady, turning to Tink, smiling. She was almost as pretty as Tink's mother. She gave Tink a key. "You will use locker number three-three-six. When you come Saturday I'll show you how we do things here. If you wonder about anything, you can ask me."

Tink took the key.

Miss Grainger turned back to Tink's mother. "There's just one thing more. The older girls wear black. The juniors wear pink leotards and slippers."

Tink nearly fainted with happiness. "Pink, Mom," she whispered.

Her mother laughed. "I give up. It was meant to be. You win. I'll get the pink whatevers you need."

"Mom," said Tink as they went downstairs and outside, "everything is funny. Yesterday I was in the most terrible tangle of my whole life. But today things are great. Maybe having red hair isn't unlucky."

"At last!" said her mother. "You're getting the idea. Having red hair is just you being you."

"And me being me *means* red hair—"

"And good ideas," said her mother, "that you'll think about."

"Even if you colored my hair, it would still really be red," said Tink.

"Right," said her mother.

"So I'm going to have to get used to red hair," said Tink.

"I can see I'm raising one smart kid," said her mother.

The bus came. They got on and the doors swooshed shut behind them.

"I've got this great idea," said Tink as they found seats.

"I'm listening," said her mother.

"When I grow up I'm going to be a ballet dancer," said Tink.

"Good idea!" said her mother.

"I'm going to dance on television," said Tink, "and be rich and famous. I'm always going to wear pink. And I'll buy you a pink dress."

"I can hardly wait," said her mother, laughing.